INDIGO WARRIORS

THE ADVENTURE BEGINS!

BY *CATHERINE JAMES*

ILLUSTRATED BY BILLIE HASTIE

KIDS
Hubble & Hattie

The Hubble & Hattie imprint was launched in 2009, and is named in memory of two very special Westie sisters owned by Veloce's proprietors. Since the first book, many more have been added, all with the same objective: to be of real benefit to the species they cover; at the same time promoting compassion, understanding and respect between all animals (including human ones!)

In 2017, the first Hubble & Hattie Kids! book – *Worzel says hello! Will you be my friend?* – was published, and has subsequently been joined by many more.

Our new range of books for kids will champion the same values and standards that we've always held dear, but to the adults of the future. Children will love reading, or having these beautifully illustrated, carefully crafted publications read to them, absorbing valuable life lessons whilst being highly entertained. We've more great books already in the pipeline so remember to check out our website for details.

Also from Hubble&Hattie kids!

Worzel says hello! Will you be my friend? (by Catherine Pickles, illustrated by Chantal Bourgonje)

Worzel goes for a walk! Will you come too? (by Catherine Pickles, illustrated by Chantal Bourgonje)

The Lucky, Lucky Leaf – A Horace and Nim Story (by Chantal Bourgonje and David Hoskins, illustrated by Chantal Bourgonje)

Positive thinking for Piglets – A Horace and Nim Story (by Chantal Bourgonje and David Hoskins, illustrated by Chantal Bourgonje)

Fierce Grey Mouse (written and illustrated by Chantal Bourgonje)

The Wandering Wildebeest (by Martin Coleman, illustrated by Tim Slater)

The Adventures of Lily and the Little Lost Doggie (written and illustrated by Laura Hamilton)

The Little House that didn't have a home (by Neil Sullivan, illustrated by Steven Burke)

My Grandad can draw anything – BUT he can't draw hands! (by Neil Sullivan, illustrated by Steven Burke)

www.hubbleandhattie.com

First published in September 2019 by Veloce Publishing Limited, Veloce House, Parkway Farm Business Park, Middle Farm Way, Poundbury, Dorchester DT1 3AR, England. Tel +44 (0)1305 260068 / Fax 01305 250479 / e-mail info@veloce.co.uk / web www.veloce.co.uk or www.velocebooks.com. ISBN: 978-1-787114-30-2; UPC: 6-36847-01430-8.
© 2019 Catherine James and Veloce Publishing.
All images, including the front panel illustration, © Billie Hastie 2019.
The author would like it known that neither she nor this work has any association with any organisation, website or media that uses the name Indigo Warrior(s).
Suggested reading age: 8-12 years, older school age readers.

CONTENTS

Chapter 1

AN ANGEL IN THE ATTIC

Jet McSwiney suspects that her guardian angel might be a bit lazy. As far as she can tell, it is made of pure, diamond-white light: nothing else. Yet it moves and sways, as fragile as a soap bubble caught in the breeze. Then there are the stars; hundreds of them. Tiny silver stars that flash and disappear all around it, like sparklers on bonfire night. Jet's angel is, by far, the most beautiful thing that she has ever seen. But it isn't always helpful and, sometimes, it is downright incompetent.

"Just my luck to have a guardian angel that can't seem to do anything right," she thinks, squinting at the angel-light that is beaming out from the corner with eye-scorching brightness. When the sparkles turn into multi-coloured blobs that float up and down, like the wax in a lava lamp, Jet arches her eyebrows.

"Oh well, now you're just showing off," she says out loud, a hand shielding her eyes, and her voice breaking into a giggle as the angel-light fades and then disappears, leaving Jet alone in the dark.

Most of the time, Jet lives a solitary life in her small, barely furnished, attic bedroom at the topmost part of the house, far away from everyone. Her home-made bed is actually five wooden pallets, roughly nailed together by her father and topped with a lumpy mattress so full of holes that it looks as if the dog has had a chew on it. But Jet doesn't care about

4

any of that. She loves her little attic. It is her refuge. Perched on the edge of the bed, Jet is preparing for her morning meditation. Taking a moment to balance herself, she grips her toes, slides her feet onto her thighs, lets her knees flop and wriggles her bottom to get comfy. Blowing upward to clear a few strands of hair from her lashes, she takes a deep breath as her eyelids close and the world begins to melt into the distance. It doesn't last long.

Jet tuts.

Her body is relaxing but her brain seems to be in overdrive, and her inner voice is bombarding her with thoughts and images that she cannot switch off. The harder Jet tries to stop them, the more they criss-cross her mind, bouncing about like the balls in a lottery machine. It doesn't help that her father's voice is thundering up the stairs, calling her to work before she goes to school. Jet is well practiced at shutting him out. "I'll just sit here and breathe until he shouts again," she thinks, "and then I'll wait for him to … arrggh … stop thinking and concentrate. Sorry, Miss Lane, I'm doing it again!" It had been Miss Lane, a young primary school teacher, who had insisted that Jet try meditation in the first place. It was either that or constant punishments because, no matter how hard she tried, Jet could not fit into the school mould. Everybody said that her attitude was wrong, and they labelled her 'disruptive,' which, she has to admit, she was. When Jet's father wanted her to take tablets that the doctor had said would "help to keep her calm," it was Miss Lane who came to her rescue. "I am sorry, Mr McSwiney, but pills are not the answer, and I really must insist that Jethro tries some meditation first – and it can't do any harm, now, can it?" the teacher had scolded Jet's dad when she stood up to him at parent's night. So far, Miss Lane is the only person ever to see through the smoke screen of Jet's unruly behaviour, and glimpse the clever, lonely girl held captive on the other side. Miss Lane had understood.

But all of that happened ages ago, when Jet was still in infant school. She has grown up a bit since then. For a start,

she no longer needs the old *Guided Meditations for Children*
CD that Miss Lane loaned to her and never got back.
Nowadays, Jet knows exactly what to do. Concentrating on
her breath, slow and deliberate … in … out … in … out, Jet
is so focused on her inner world that she misses the sound
of footsteps padding up the stairs, and when the attic door
opens, the sudden shift in her attention is gut wrenching. If
her father was to come in and catch her …!

Jet doesn't dare to think about the consequences.

But it is her mother's flushed, round face that appears
at the side of the creaky little door, her eyes showing no
affection as they scan the room before coming to rest on the
meditating child.

"Jethro," her mum hisses, without setting a foot over the
threshold. "Please, come down before your father calls again.
He's in a foul mood already this morning … don't make it
any worse for yourself."

"Yeah, worse for you, more like," thinks Jet, half opening
one eye and squinting through her fringe at her mother, who
is disappearing around the door and gently pulling it closed,
with a quiet 'click' of the latch.

"SHE'S UP, LOVE," Mrs McSwiney calls from the
landing, as much for Jet's benefit as for her father's.
"SHE'LL BE DOWN IN A MINUTE."

Ignoring her mother's plea, Jet opens both eyes, tosses
back her fringe and glances at the corner. Sunshine hardly
ever reaches Jet's window, and when it does, the beam cuts
a straight line into the room, revealing every splinter and
gap in the floorboards, but missing the cold little corner
altogether. Right now it is illuminated by the white sparkling
light of her protector. Jet can never work out why her angel
chooses a particular time to appear in her bedroom. It comes
and goes as it pleases.

"Oh, you're back, are you!" she snaps, irritated at yet
another interruption, "If you are my guardian angel, how
come you don't do anything to help me … hmmm? After all
… that IS supposed to be your job … isn't it?"

Flickering at the intensity of Jet's hostility, the angel-light shrinks a little, but it makes no sound. It never does.

"Concentrate," Jet mutters, scolding herself, her eyelids closing with some force, "and for goodness sake, visualise!" A few moments later, after several short, shallow breaths, Jet finds herself drifting into a sunlit meadow filled with sweet-scented flowers of every possible colour. She is enjoying the warm, imagined sunshine, when it is eclipsed by four squabbling children, who jostle and shove their way into her vision. Two boys and two girls cast long black shadows as they try to materialise on the grass in front of her. The grainy image is wobbling like an out-of-focus home video, but Jet can see that the children are quarrelling, really quite savagely. Unable to hear their voices, she has no idea what they might be arguing about. They seem innocent enough. Squinting into the sunshine, she watches the children with a lazy interest, the way she might gaze at a television screen. It is only when they look back, and, seeming to notice her, move forward until their faces almost fill the screen, that Jet flinches. Startled, she wonders if they can actually see her. But how could they? She imagined them. They don't exist. They're not real ... are they?

The taller of the boys frowns, raising a hand to point his index finger before nudging the other boy and then signalling to the girls to look into the distance. Eyes wide and not looking the least bit brave, the four children shrink back as they stare ... at what? Then vague movements, like reflections in a shop window, draw Jet's attention to a fifth figure, an outsider that seems to be lurking on the very edge of her vision, keeping its distance from the others. How could she have missed it? Jet's eyes move quickly under their closed lids, but it is no use because, whatever this creature is, it cannot fully materialise, and its shadowy grey face reminds her of the man in the moon. A shudder shoots up Jet's spine and her breaths speed up, as a smothering sadness pours over her until she feels that she might drown in it. Tears rim her eyelids, then a sharp pain and the metallic taste of her own blood tells her that she has bitten through her lip. Jet shivers.

Within seconds her whole body is quivering uncontrollably and she can stand it no longer. Scrunching her eyes tight, she shakes her head as hard as she can and, in an instant, the vision is gone. Snapping her eyelids open, Jet whirls her head around to face the angel in the corner.

"Who on earth were that lot?" she demands, a dry mouth making her voice break. "How did they even get into my imagination … and that horrible … faceless … thing … what was all that about?" The flickering angel-light throbs and sparkles as if nothing had happened and Jet receives no guidance: no insights, no ideas or intuitions. "Are they indigo children? Tell me … in here!" she presses her finger to her forehead before answering her own question, "No! They couldn't be. They look too ordinary for that." Taking a long, calming breath, Jet considers the children for a moment, but they don't really interest her, and concentrating on that creepy outsider has made her brain ache as if it is stuffed into a skull three sizes too small.

"JETHRO MCSWINEY, GET DOWN HERE." Her father's voice bursts into the air, shattering her thoughts. Knowing, from past experience, that her beautiful meadow cannot be recreated, at least not today, Jet uncoils her legs, stretches and looks around her drab little bedroom. The angel-light has vanished.

"I'M COMING!" she shouts and then mutters, "He can't even see you, for goodness sake … what kind of guardian angel does a runner at the first sign of my dad?"

"JETHRO MCSWINEY!" Her father's voice blasts up the stairs. "Get down here RIGHT NOW! There's farm work to be done. MOVE IT!"

"OKAY, JUST COMING," Jet calls, distractedly, her thoughts returning to the four children that she has just imagined. Did her own brain conjure them up from nowhere … to trick her? It wouldn't be the first time. Could it be a vision of the future? She hasn't had that before. Picking up her purple hand mirror, Jet absentmindedly moves her fingers over the pointed wings of a plastic dragon, draped across the top, its jagged tail wrapped around the glass, as if protecting it. "No," she thinks, holding the dragon up to her face to inspect her bitten lip in the mirror. "But then, why would that work-shy angel even bother to show them to me ... and what about that faceless outsider ... thing?"

Jet shudders.

She wonders when – or if – the universe will bring these four seemingly ordinary kids into her life. But she can't think of a single reason why it would bother to do that, and, right now, she really doesn't have time to worry about it.

"I'M ALMOST READY," she calls to her father, fearing the penalty for ignoring his commands and keen to avoid another battle with her parents.

Picking up her mud-caked wellingtons, she slowly pulls on one boot, pausing to dab a trickle of blood from her lip before pulling on the other. Her father's voice roars from the ground floor.

"DON'T MAKE ME COME UP THOSE STAIRS, MY GIRL!"

"ON MY WAY," shouts Jet, trying to sound light-hearted. Stepping through the attic door, she turns to take one last look at her beloved little bedroom, trying to physically absorb the sheer calmness of her sanctuary. Then, summoning all of her strength, Jet turns away, and is pulling the door behind her when a powerful force knocks her off balance, sweeping her towards the steep wooden stairwell and almost toppling her, head first, down the stairs. Grabbing for the banister, she sways over the top step, her toes hanging over the edge. Taking a moment to steady herself, Jet forces her lips into a half-hearted smile before going down to face her parents. They would never understand.

"For heaven's sake, take it easy, okay," she scolds her guardian angel, because she is convinced that it has just tried, rather clumsily, to give her a nudge. Then an unsettling thought flashes into her head: "Enjoy it while you can, Indigo Girl, because Planet Earth needs your help. Get ready to fight back."

Chapter 2

A TREE AT THE END OF THE ROAD

At the end of an extra hard training session Noah Fitzroy spins his green sports wheelchair one hundred and eighty degrees, and heads along the road towards Peter Fairchild's house. He skipped breakfast this morning and his stomach is starting to grumble. Running on empty, Noah's tired muscles really ache, and his fringe is stuck flat against his forehead. Warm sweat trickles from the back of his neck, cooling by the time it reaches the waistband of his leggings. The wheel rims are so hot that Noah can feel the heat through his gloves, but his wheelchair never lets him down: jumping, spinning, and flipping when he performs acrobatics at the skateboarding arena in the park. But not today. It is speed that Noah needs today because he is in a hurry. He is on a mission.

Heading round to the back of Peter's mum's council house, Noah pushes on the high wooden gate, which opens a little and then sticks on the uneven slabs. Gritting his teeth, he slips off his gloves before delicately rolling his chair this way and that: easing himself through the narrow gap, grating his knuckles on the rough weathered wood.

"Oh, for pete's sake, when are they going to get this bloomin' gate fixed," he mutters, inspecting the scratches on the back of his hands before looking up. "Oh, err … sorry, I …"

The tiny back garden is crammed full of pink-faced people, all balanced on one leg and contorted into extremely improbable shapes. For a fraction of a second they all stand completely still, looking in Noah's direction. But the screech of the gate has set Peter's mum's teeth on edge, and she shudders and sways before spread-eagling onto the spongy, moss-ridden, grass. Their concentration shattered, her yoga students collapse around her like a pyramid of acrobats, hitting the ground in a tangled heap of multi-coloured legs, arms and bodies.

"Sorry, Mrs Fairchild," says Noah, "I'm looking for Peter."

"He's over there ... somewhere," says Mrs Fairchild, smiling up at Noah from the ground, and waving a hand in the general direction of the far corner. Miss Carver, the delicatessen lady, is helping Peter to untangle his limbs when his mouth breaks into a wide, grateful smile.

"Noah! Fantastic!" he calls, adding, "Sorry, Mum, I just need to go and ... erm ..."

Stony-faced, Mrs Fairchild kneels on her yoga mat, crosses her arms and glares at Peter as he gathers his things before picking his way through the tangle of bodies and disappearing into the kitchen. Noah wastes no time in following Peter into the house.

"Hell's bells, Pete," says Noah, stifling a laugh. "What are you doing? You don't do yoga ... or maybe you do ... secretly."

"Don't start, Noah," snaps Peter, lifting piles of clothes and sports bags to clear a path through the hall to the living room. "The church hall is closed this afternoon so Mum brought her beginners' class here for practice – and before you say anything, she insisted that I join in – you know what she's like."

Noah nods, but says nothing because he does know what Peter's mum is like. When they were little boys, Peter often went hungry whilst his mum danced or sat on a cushion, chanting for hours on end.

"Children," she would say to them, in a flurry of cheesecloth and purple fringes. "Life is far too short to waste your time doing things that you hate." Mrs Fairchild was often so busy learning some new fad or other that she completely forgot Peter was even there. But he won't hear a word said against her. "She enjoys life," is what he tells people, when they say that she neglects him.

"Have you eaten?" asks Noah.

"Well, there wasn't really time," says Peter. "I'll get something when they've gone. It's fine."

"It's not fine," says Noah, pointedly. "You must be hungry. Look, why don't you come to mine for tea? Stay the night. Esther's going out with Mum – thankfully – and my dad's doing his special home-made pizza. Fancy?"

"Oh, I don't know …" says Peter, glancing at a large shopping trolley propped against an untidy guinea pig pen. "I had planned to go into town today."

"You can do that tomorrow," says Noah, interrupting him, "nobody can resist my dad's super-pizza, and I know you must be starving. Anyway, there's something I need to show you. Come on."

"Okay," says Peter, pulling off a pair of his mum's bright orange leggings, and reaching for his jeans, "just let me get changed and I'll need to bring my trolley with me."

"Great," says Noah, doing a three point turn and heading towards the door. "My dad'll put some stuff in it for you."

"You're really awful about your sister, you know," says Peter, trundling his trolley behind him, as they make their way along the road towards Noah's street. "She's not that bad, and she's only five."

Noah rolls his eyes.

"Not that bad!" he says. "Are you kidding? She is SO bossy, and she barges into my room all the time. She's really annoying."

"Oh, really?" says Peter, raising his eyebrows and looking sideways at Noah. "You don't say."

* * * * *

The boys find Noah's dad in the family's clinically spotless kitchen. He is hunched over the worktop, engrossed in chopping tomatoes for his speciality dish of thin crispy pizza served with fat potato wedges. He flashes a broad friendly smile when he sees the boys.

"Hello Peter, how's the food collecting going?" he says, rinsing his hands before opening the wall cupboard and taking out a few ring pull cans and packets of biscuits that he drops into Peter's trolley.

"Hey, Mr Fitzroy," says Peter. "Pretty good, thanks. Everybody seems to be really generous."

"Well, I hope those homeless people appreciate what you do for them … here, have these as well," says Mr Fitzroy, unhooking a bunch of bananas from a gleaming chrome hanger and handing them to Peter. "Are you sure you're safe going down those alleys with this stuff? Don't you get scared?"

"No. People are all right, really. I don't worry too much about that," says Peter, not quite telling the truth. "As long as they get something to eat, I'm happy, you know?"

Mr Fitzroy's smile broadens.

"Yes, Peter," he says, his head tilting and bobbing in a sideways nod. "I do."

At dinner time the boys take their pizzas to Noah's specially adapted bedroom, where they devour the food and then abandon their trays wherever they can find a space amongst discarded clothes and books. Nobody is allowed to touch Noah's stuff, and tidying up is never his priority. Years ago, the council installed a shower room and, at the Occupational Therapist's insistence, a fire door that opens from the bedroom directly onto a metal ramp that Noah doesn't actually need.

Reaching to the floor, Noah picks up a sweater and pulls it over his training vest.

"Aren't you going to shower?" asks Peter. "You're a bit sweaty."

Noah shrugs.

"Jeez," says Peter, flopping onto the little corduroy sofa and tearing open an enormous bag of popcorn, getting ready to watch a movie. "You said you wanted to ask me something."

"Yeah, look at this," says Noah, rummaging about under some magazines and handing Peter a sheet of laminated paper. "I found it nailed to that big tree at the end of the street. It says that the council wants to chop it down."

"Oh, ouch!" says Peter. "That's a shame. Why are you telling me? I can't do anything about that."

"Well, I can," says Noah, matter-of-factly. "I'm going to stop them, Pete. I'm going to sit on one of the branches until I force them to change their minds."

Popcorn sprays from Peter's mouth, shooting across the carpet like an explosion of cannon balls. Raising his eyes to the ceiling, Noah tuts loudly. When Peter has finished choking, he catches his breath and stares, wide-eyed, at his friend.

"I'm sorry, Noah, what did you just say?" he asks when he has recovered. "You're going to ... do what?"

"What's wrong with that?" says Noah, shaking his head and shrugging casually. "Everybody does it nowadays. It's the only way to stop them. Everybody knows that."

"But Noah ... how ... I mean, you can't ... well ... climb," says Peter, nodding towards the wheelchair.

"Yes, I am aware of that, airhead," says Noah, lobbing a cushion at Peter, who heads it back to him, like a football. "Nor can I fly up there, but that's where you come in."

"Oh, gawd ... is it?" says Peter, suspiciously, a handful of popcorn held static in front of his face, ready to be fired into his mouth. "Go on then ... tell me what you want me to do?"

"Well, we can do a poster campaign to let people know about the tree being cut down," says Noah, enthusiastically. "You're good at design so you can make all the posters."

"Okay," says Peter, half smiling at Noah being bossy, as usual.

"And," Noah continues, "you can borrow a rope and harnesses from your climbing club and bring them round here."

"Okay, then what?" asks Peter, who is genuinely interested. "How are you going to get yourself up the tree?"

"You can hoist me up with the rope," says Noah, confidently.

"WHAT!" exclaims Peter, horrified. "Err ... No! I don't think so, Noah. I'm not strong enough for that."

"Yeah, course you are," says Noah, breezily, carefully avoiding eye contact with Peter. "It'll be fine. Trust me ... be great ... honest."

Peter groans, his body slumping into the sofa, head against the backrest, his face tilted towards the ceiling.

"One condition, Noah," he says. "We try the simple approach first. We'll hand out some leaflets in the town and, if we can get public support from that, then you don't go up the tree. Agreed?"

"No! Not agreed! That's just wasting time!" snaps Noah. "For pete's sake, Pete, leafleting won't do any good. How will that be any good?"

"Well, we do that first or I'm out," says Peter, picking up his popcorn bag and taking another fistful towards his mouth. "I mean it, Noah. OUT!"

"Right!" says Noah, angrily, "Right, have it your way. We'll try the posters and leaflets first, even though we both know that it won't do any good."

The door is flung open and Esther skips into the bedroom, wearing her favourite lemon party frock and singing cheerfully, at the top of her voice.

"I'm ba- a- ck. Oh, hello Peter ... "

"WE'RE BUSY!" barks Noah, so forcefully that Esther makes a hasty retreat, running down the hall in tears and calling for her mum.

Peter shakes his head.

* * * * *

On Saturday morning, the boys meet on the ground floor of the busiest shopping centre in town. Positioning themselves next to the sports emporium at the bottom of the escalator, they plan to spend the whole day handing out their 'Save Our Tree' leaflets. Cringing at the loudness of the mall music, Noah secures the brakes on his chair whilst Peter sets his trolley aside, slips off his backpack and drops it to the ground. Plunging his hand into its depths, he rummages amongst his provisions. Noah looks on, impatiently, as a water bottle is placed on the ground, then a bag of crisps and some chocolate. A comb and a book. A set of headphones. Finally Peter pulls out the bundle of home-made leaflets and drops half of them onto Noah's lap.

"This will do the trick, Noah," he says. "Once people hear about your tree, they're bound to do something to save it."

Blinding lights blaze down on determined shoppers, who criss-cross the concourse, pushing and shoving as they run from one store to the next. They all give the boys a wide berth, practically tiptoeing around them, and deliberately averting their eyes to avoid catching their attention. Nobody is interested in their campaign, and nobody wants a leaflet.

Grabbing hold of Peter's rucksack, Noah rips it open with such force that the zipper almost comes off the end. He fires his bundle of leaflets into the bag.

"They just don't understand, Noah," says Peter, sympathetically. "It's not their fault. I'm really sorry …"

"What is there to understand, Pete?" says Noah, exasperated at what he considers to be a general lack of intelligence. "We've been here for two hours and not one leaflet has been accepted. Not one! They just don't care!"

"What about taking the leaflets into school on Monday," says Peter, eager to direct Noah away from his idea of going up the tree.

"And just why would we even bother to do that, Pete, hmm?" says Noah, sneeringly. "School kids aren't going to be any better informed than this lot of morons."

"Well what then?" says Peter. "I don't know what else we can do."

When he spots a uniformed security guard picking his way through the dense crowd, heading in their direction, Peter quickly throws his belongings into the rucksack and flips one of the straps over his right shoulder.

"Idiots!" Noah is shouting at the top of his voice, "Sleepwalkers! Robots! This is important!"

"Shut up, Noah," snaps Peter, grasping the handle of his trolley. "There's a security man watching us and I think he's coming over ... we'd better get out of here."

"But we don't have much time left," says Noah, grasping the wheel rims on his chair so forcefully that his knuckles turn white. "They'll kill that tree if I don't do something. I told you this was useless. I told you! But, oh no, you wouldn't listen, would you? We need to take acti..."

"I know!" snaps Peter, cutting him off, as they hurry towards the exit and out of the arcade before the guard can catch up with them. "Come on, we have a lot to do ... and stop moaning!"

* * * * *

The following evening, in Noah's bedroom, the boys draw up their plan to save the tree. At first they consider picketing the council offices, but dismiss the idea immediately, since two pickets wouldn't really make much of an impression.

"We could nobble the council vehicles," offers Noah, "let down the tyres or something."

Peter stares at him, his eyes wide and eyebrows wrinkling into an astonished frown.

"Well, what then?" snaps Noah. "Look, either you come up with a better idea, or I'm going up that tree – whether you like it or not."

Peter considers the problem until his head hurts, but he just can't think of a workable strategy. Left with no other choice, he agrees to help Noah put his plan into action.

"At bloomin' last," says Noah, "some common sense. Let's get to work."

Over the next few days Peter borrows a rope, helmets and climbing harnesses from his sports club. His little nylon rucksack is stuffed with some biscuits, a carton of juice, a box of plasters, some tissues and a bundle of the leaflets. Then everything is pushed under Noah's bed: hidden from Esther, who has no respect for a closed bedroom door and would buckle immediately if anyone questioned her about the boys' activities.

Then … nothing.

Noah's patience is tested to the limit, because it is three weeks later, whilst he is poring over yet another bundle of mind-numbing newspapers, that he finds it: the date for the tree felling is reported in a tiny column, on the back page of a local paper, in a corner, under the football results.

"Gotcha!" he says, his hand automatically shooting under the heap of crumpled newspapers on his desk, feeling about for his phone.

* * * * *

The night before the tree is to be cut down, Peter sleeps over at Noah's house, as usual, and the boys are awake before sunrise. Tripping over one another, they tiptoe about the dark little bedroom, working by the light from their torches, and desperately trying not to disturb Noah's family. Reaching under the bed, Peter drags the equipment into the middle of the room and begins to sort through it, separating it into two piles. Passing a climbing harness to Noah, he prepares to step into his own, and he is balancing on one leg, the other one being half way through a leg loop on his harness, when Noah hits a snag.

"It's caught on the chair somewhere," he whispers.

"I'll get it for you," says Peter, lowering his own harness to the floor before grasping the strap on Noah's, and giving it a good tug. "Lift your body so I can see where it's jammed … a bit more … I can't see it."

"I am lifting," says Noah, "... just pull it, for pete's sake!"

"I can't!" says Peter. "Try rolling to the right so that I can free this bit."

"I'm rolling," says Noah, shifting his weight onto one side of his bottom. "Can't you get it? Hurry up."

"Wait a minute ... if I pull on this ... " says Peter, yanking the thick webbing strap, suddenly freeing it, and almost catapulting Noah right out of the wheelchair.

"Oh, for pete's sake!" hisses Noah, grabbing the side of the chair to stop himself from falling out.

"Shush," snaps Peter, "you'll wake ... "

Click.

Light flashes under the bedroom door, casting a moving shadow of feet walking up the hall. A thin, wail of a yawn disturbs the silence as soft soled slippers drag along the laminate floor, padding towards the bathroom. Esther is up.

Immediately flicking off their torches, the boys freeze. Noah folds his arms across his chest, convinced that Peter must be able to hear the beat of his heart, thudding inside his rib cage. If Esther comes in now, it's game over for sure, and his tree will be lost forever.

The toilet flushes, the light switch clicks and Esther's footsteps are back in the hall. They shuffle towards Noah's bedroom door ... stop ... shuffle a few more ... stop again ... the brass door handle is pressed down.

Noah and Peter wait perfectly still, eyes fixed on each other. Noah can barely breathe because the success, or failure, of his plan is hanging on whatever his little sister decides to do next.

Esther lets out a long weary sigh, the handle flips up and her footsteps change direction as she turns towards her own room. The boys listen for the click of the bedroom door handle, before breathing out. Then, out of the darkness, Noah hears Peter sniggering and stifling a laugh.

"What was funny about that?" says Noah, angrily, flicking on his torch and holding it up to his face. "I could have fallen out of my chair, or we could have been caught. We almost got caught!"

"Oh, stop complaining, Noah," says Peter. "You never fall out of your chair! Imagine what Esther would have thought if she had walked in and seen us here? Look at the state of us … standing in the dark like a couple of would-be rebels. Even you have to admit that it's a bit mad."

"Mad it may be," says Noah, high-handedly, "but it is not the least bit funny. Now can we move along, please?"

At last, Noah, wearing a bright purple climbing harness and dayglow skateboarding gear, is ready for the battle to save his tree. Feeling like a super-human shield, he truly is prepared to defend the whole of Planet Earth … single-handed if need be.

"Ready?" asks Peter, hoping that the answer will be 'no'.

"Bring it on," says Noah, spinning his chair and leading the way through his fire door, down the ramp and into the back garden.

Here and there, breaks in the cloud allow the moon to peek through and cast long black shadows onto the grass. Dark green shrubs spread out like fingers reaching for the paved path on which stands a small barbecue, whose cover has never been removed since it was bought, two summers ago. There is a chill in the air and, stopping for a moment, the boys look around the garden, taking in the atmosphere.

"This had better be worth it," hisses Peter. "I've never been out of my bed at this time of night, let alone standing outside in a flaming garden. I'm freezing! Why did I let you talk me into this?"

"I know," whispers Noah, adjusting the collar on his fleece and turning his chair towards the back gate. "It's a nightmare. Come on, let's just get on with it."

Grateful that there is no sign of life anywhere on the street, the boys start along the eerily deserted pavement. The dim orange glow of the street lights smudges grey pre-dawn colours, so that they run into one another like watery

paints on a canvas. Curtains are drawn in every darkened window and the only witness to the boys' activities is Hercules, the swaggering young tabby cat from number 29. His curiosity getting the better of him, Hercules slips out from his hiding place under a hedge and pads behind the boys, stalking them as they hurry towards the tree at the end of the road.

Positioning his wheelchair directly under its branches, Noah secures the brakes and looks straight up at the long five-finger leaves, fluttering high above him. Letting out a gasp, he realises, for the first time, just how tall 'his' tree really is and he can feel his hands starting to tremble. His thoughts race so much that he has trouble remembering how to tie the bowline knot, to attach the rope to his harness. Quickly repeating the instructions – "… rabbit down the hole … out the hole … round the tree … down the hole …" – he just can't make it work, and the first tinge of panic flashes through his body.

"Take it easy, Noah, I'll make sure it's fastened," says Peter, as he ties the knot, double checks that it is secure and then nods.

This time neither boy is laughing.

Setting his trolley aside, Peter carefully prepares the rope and throws it over one of the branches. The boys look at the height of the tree and then at each other.

"Hell's bells, Noah," says Peter. "I really hope this holds."

"Oh, this tree won't let me come to any harm," says Noah, his hand running over the rough bark, which catches his thumb. "Ouch!"

"Noah. It's a tree," says Peter. "It can't … oh, never mind. Are you ready for this?"

"Nope," murmurs Noah, under his breath, bracing himself before he looks at Peter, smiles and gives a single nod.

"Right! Well, here goes nothing," says Peter, taking up the slack and pulling the rope through the braking plate on his harness: heaving Noah out of his wheelchair.

Suspended on the end of the rope, Noah slowly makes his way up the tree, using his muscular arms to pull himself along the trunk and taking care to avoid looking down at the hard tarmac pavement, far below.

Flicking his head, Peter blinks away some sweat that drips from his fringe, only to catch on his lashes and run into his eyes, stinging them. He hasn't lifted such a heavy weight before, and the grueling effort is straining his muscles so much that he feels they might be ripped away from his bones. To prevent the rope from pulling him upward, he sits back, as hard as he can, in the climbing harness, his shoes scuffing the pavement as he struggles to keep his feet on the ground.

Noah is almost half way up the tree when a faint groan comes from the branch. Acting on instinct, Peter stops pulling.

"Don't stop now!" says Noah, his voice going quite high, as he jerks to a halt, dangling on the end of the rope. "What'd you think you're doing?"

"The branch creaked," says Peter. "I don't think it's going to hold."

"Just keep going," pleads Noah. "For pete's sake … keep going!"

Summoning all of his strength, Peter pulls the rope and Noah climbs a few slow centimetres. The groaning branch suddenly creaks and bends, instantly dropping Noah as if a trap door has opened under him. In a split second, Peter has lost control of the rope, plunging Noah towards the pavement at lightning speed. Noah scrambles to grab for the tree, but he can't reach because the rope is pulling him away. His wrists drag across the bark, tearing at his skin until it is scraped and bloody. The rope rips through Peter's fingers, burning them, as he fights to gain control of Noah's fall, and, when he finally does, Noah is just one metre away from hitting the pavement.

As quickly as he can, Peter lowers Noah back to the safety of his wheelchair and, holding his smarting hands in his armpits, takes in a long, quivering, breath before he can speak.

"Noah, I really don't think we should be ..."

"Try the next one up, if you can reach it," says Noah, "and hurry."

"Stop ordering me about, Noah!" snaps Peter, "I'm doing it, okay!"

Concentrating, Peter holds the rope like a lasso and flings it up to a higher branch. Missed. Recoiling the rope, he tries again. Missed.

"*I can't do this*," he thinks, despair washing over him like an ice cold wave: his hands are throbbing from rope burns and Noah, his best friend, is depending on him. "*I'm just not strong enough ... I wish somebody ... anybody ... could help me!*"

Breathing deeply, Peter takes a moment to slow the pumping beat of his heart. Spreading his feet to stabilise himself, he turns his head to the side, allowing his gaze to drift upwards, drawn to a sphere of electric blue light that is orbiting a branch, high in the tree. Half closing his eyes and squinting at the brightness of the light against the night sky, Peter is transfixed.

Before he knows what is happening, his arm has extended and he has thrown the rope, dream-like, towards the light. As if in slow motion, the rope flies high into the air and sails, effortlessly, over the branch. As it travels through the light, the neon glow seems to stick to it, like phosphorous on the surface of the ocean, and when the end of the rope tumbles down into Peter's hands, they, too, start to glow as he feels his strength returning, the pain subsiding.

"Okay," he says, robotically, turning to look at Noah through glazed, staring eyes. "One more try."

Pulling the rope rigid, Peter lifts Noah out of his wheelchair and hauls him back up the tree. This time the sturdy branch, now pulsing vivid blue, does not complain. Moments later Noah is clambering onto the branch and wrapping his safety rope around it. Feeling pleased with himself, he gives Peter a double thumbs up, completely unaware of the fluorescent glow that is pulsing, almost breathing, all around him. Peter stares until the light begins to fade, gradually thinning to a wisp before disappearing altogether.

Noah is impatient.

"Oi … can you hear me? … I said we did it!" he calls down to Peter. "Didn't I tell you it would be okay?"

"What … yeah …" murmurs Peter, unsure of what has just happened to him and deciding not to tell Noah. "Yeah … we, erm … did it."

Dawn is lighting the sky when Peter ties the little rucksack onto the rope and signals to Noah to pull it up. Then the lightweight wheelchair is folded, hauled up, and fixed with bungee cords, dangling from the branch, for maximum effect. Finally, Noah pulls the rope up like a drawbridge and he is on his own. He is ready to make his protest.

"You'd better make yourself scarce, Pete," he says. "I'll phone you if I need you."

Peter says nothing. In a daze, he waves to Noah, picks up the handle of his shopping trolley, and heads into town to give a breakfast of out-of-date bagels, soft pitted apples, tea biscuits, and tinned peaches to some people who live on the streets.

* * * * *

Noah is developing a stinker of a mood when, after spending hours sitting on an uncomfortable branch, he finally spots a council van with three workmen in the front, turning into the street.

"At last," he says and then gulps. "Oh no, I guess this is it, then."

Too busy to notice Noah sitting high above him, a small workman opens the back door of the van, drags out a large orange chainsaw, balances it on his knee, adjusts his grip on the handle, and then slides it down his leg, onto the pavement. Noah watches him pull and re-pull the starter cord until, roaring like the throttle of a motorcycle, the powerful chainsaw thunders into life. It looks enormous in the man's thin little hands and he struggles to lift it. Noah shouts, but he is startled when the workman doesn't hear him above the noise of the saw. He hadn't thought of that.

"*Oh no,*" he thinks, panic rushing through him again. "*They can't hear me. They're going to cut this thing down with me still in it.*"

Desperately cupping his hands around his mouth to make a megaphone, Noah starts to bawl at the top of his voice.

"HELP! HELP!" he shouts. "LOOK UP, YOU MORONS. LOOK UP!"

Busily closing the road for the job of chopping down the tree, the workmen throw down lines of red and white cones and then set out signs to redirect the traffic. But they still don't hear Noah, and they do not look up. Digging into the pocket of his fleece Noah feels for his phone. The pocket is empty. He pats around his body. All pockets are empty. Frantically plunging his hands into the rucksack he fumbles amongst the provisions, searching for his phone – nothing.

"Oh, you blathering idiot," he mutters, a lightning bolt shooting up his spine as he remembers that he left his phone, attached to the charger, on his desk. "What am I going to do now?"

Dropping a leaflet, Noah watches it flutter down and land just in front of the burly foreman, who unwittingly mashes it into the ground under his steel capped boot. The small workman finally manages to lift the buzzing chainsaw, the power of the machine pushing him so hard that he staggers backwards for almost two metres. In desperation, Noah drops another leaflet, willing the foreman to see it. But he doesn't notice that one either. Finally gaining control of the chainsaw, the small workman thuds it against the tree, ready to sink the rotating blade into the thick, gnarled bark.

"HEY! UP HERE!" Noah waves his arms about in a panic. "For pete's sake look up! PLEASE LOOK UP!"

In desperation he flings the bundle of leaflets high into the air and watches them swirl to the ground like a snow storm. Surrounded by a flurry of twirling paper the foreman looks up to see Noah, perched on the branch, grinning with relief, a hand raised and fingers wriggling in a cheeky wave.

"STOP THAT SAW!" shouts the foreman. "There's someone in the flaming tree."

"What the …?" The suddenness of the command startles the small workman so much that he completely loses control of the saw, and the powerful kick-back from the machine makes him stagger around, with the blade waving all over the place.

"Mind what you're doing, you idiot," says the bigger workman.

"Turn it off, you fool. Turn it off," shouts the foreman.

"I can't," says the small workman. "Get out of the way. Woaaaah."

Seeming to have a life of its own, the vibrating machine flails around with the terrified workman hanging on to the end of it. The purple faced foreman, whose veins are sticking out on his forehead, is beginning to froth at the mouth.

"Right," he says, his voice hoarse with rage, "that's it! Let's not mess about with this flaming protester! I'm calling the police!"

Secretly smiling to one another, the two workmen put down their tools, settle themselves in the van and open an enormous flask of tea.

After fifteen minutes, PC Dally turns into the street on his motorcycle. Dismounting, the policeman takes a moment to adjust the belt on his yellow high-vis jacket. Then he takes off his helmet and places it, carefully, on the saddle before sauntering across the street.

"There's a kid in the tree," says the foreman, pointing up at Noah. "We can't cut it down with a flaming kid in it."

The easy-going policeman smiles, speaks quietly into his radio and then sighs.

"Now then, lad," he shouts up to Noah. "The game's over. You've had your fun. Be sensible and come down. Good lord, is that a wheelchair up there?"

"No way," shouts Noah. "I've never been more sensible

in my life. I want to save this tree from being cut down and I'm staying put."

PC Dally smiles at Noah, his eyelid flicking a quick secret wink. Then he switches off his radio and looks at the foreman.

"Well?" he says.

"But it's a hazard to the road users," says the foreman, exasperated.

"You have to admit that its branches do obscure the traffic lights," says PC Dally, reasonably. "We can't ignore that, son."

"Yes, I know that," says Noah, "but we can't keep chopping down trees everywhere. We need to find another way to fix this."

"There isn't another way," says the foreman, waving a piece of paper in the air. "I've got a council order here … the tree's got to come down, so get your backside out of it. NOW!"

"No way!" says Noah, closing his eyes, his hand making a long, theatrical, swipe in the air.

"Hmmm," says the policeman, coughing to conceal a laugh. "We seem to be having a stand-off here. I'll contact the council. Shall I find out what they want us to … err … do … so to speak."

Whistling cheerily, PC Dally strolls back to his motorcycle to make the call in private, whilst an increasing number of bystanders gather on the pavement under the tree. Noah drops his remaining leaflets, but the crowd tramples them into the pavement, along with the others.

"I came up here to save this tree," he shouts, hoping to rally support for his cause.

"Why?" asks a voice from the crowd. "It's only a tree."

"We shouldn't cut down trees just because we feel like it," shouts Noah. "This tree was here before we were, and it will still be here long after we've gone."

"So what?" says the voice.

"SO WHAT!" shouts Noah, waving a fist so forcefully that

he loses his grip, almost slipping from the branch. "This tree has a right to be left alone."

"Bleedin' nutcase," says someone in the crowd.

"I'm off to work," says another.

The stand-off is broken when a gleaming chauffeur-driven car, with blacked-out windows, crawls around the corner and parks behind the council van. Struggling to squeeze his huge body through the door, Councillor Beattie clambers out, wheezing and complaining about missing a good breakfast at his golf club. Noah can't help sniggering as the councillor waddles towards the tree like an over-inflated beach ball on legs, the polished leather on his smart black shoes creaking under the strain.

"Now, look here, little fellow," says the councillor, loftily. "I am Councillor Beattie. I am a very important person in these parts, and I've got very important work to do, so you'd better come down, right now … or I'll make them come up and fetch you down."

"I'm not fetching him," says the small workman.

"Me neither," says the other workman.

"You have to admit the boy has a point," says the foreman.

"NO! He does NOT!" shouts Councillor Beattie, spinning around to stand nose to nose with the foreman. "That tree is coming down … TODAY! Do I make myself clear?"

"Well, you'll have to cut me down with it," says Noah, his natural bravado returning.

When his parents join the crowd, Esther, perched unsteadily on her dad's shoulders, is pointing up at the tree and shouting, "that's my big brother up there … he's a superhero, you know."

"What in heavens name are you doing, Noah?" his mum calls up to him. "How did you get up there? Good grief, is that … your wheelchair? And where's Peter?"

"I'm saving this tree, Mum," says Noah. "Someone had to do it."

"Good for you, son," says his dad, kneeling down before lifting Esther over his head, and setting her on the ground.

Returning from his trip into town, Peter hides behind a blue and white campervan that is parked across the street, and settles down to watch the spectacle with some amusement. Seeing no sign of any light around the tree – blue or otherwise – he shrugs, conceding that he must have imagined it because he was over-tired from staying awake during the night.

"Come on, Councillor Beattie," says PC Dally, flatly, rubbing his forehead, and looking decidedly bored with the situation. "You need to make a decision. We're all waiting."

Councillor Beattie takes a moment to consider his options before turning to the policeman.

"Arrest him!" he says, his chubby forefinger pointing at Noah.

"Arrest him?" says Noah's dad. "Oh, my lord."

"What ... whoa?" gasps Noah, losing his balance and grabbing the tree trunk to stop himself from falling. That wasn't in his plan. Arrest him? He didn't expect that.

In his hiding place, behind the campervan, Peter closes his eyes and puts his head in his hands, afraid that he and Noah are about to be dragged off to prison.

PC Dally purses his lips.

"Hmmm," he says, "now, are you sure about that, Councillor? Arresting a disabled boy? That will sell a lot of newspapers, don't you think, Councillor?"

"Disabled?" snarls Councillor Beattie, flicking a thumb in Noah's direction. "That pest up there is more able than the rest of us put together."

"Well, yes, he is, but even so ..." says PC Dally, inclining his head toward the crowd.

Councillor Beattie's eyelids fall to half closed, and, keeping his head perfectly still, he takes a long sideways look at the voting public who have gathered to see the disabled boy in the tree.

"Oh, very well, young man," he says, grudgingly, glaring up at Noah, "I suppose you're going to tell me that you have a better idea."

"What ... oh, erm ... well ... yes, as a matter of fact I do ... erm ...," says Noah, taken by surprise.

"Well, get on with it!" snarls the Councillor. "That's why you're up there, isn't it?"

"It's simple really," says Noah. "Just trim the tree branches every year to keep the traffic lights clear. Oh ... and sweep up the leaves. That way the tree can be left in peace. You see? Everybody wins."

Petrified, Noah keeps his eyes fixed on the councillor, who is completely straight-faced. Secreted behind the campervan, with his fingers crossed, Peter holds his breath. Esther falls silent. The small crowd of bystanders fidget restlessly as the councillor makes his decision.

"Right, foreman," he shouts, turning his face to the crowd, his mouth curving into a creepy open-mouthed smile, like a Halloween pumpkin with a gold filling. "You'd better get started – trimming those branches and clearing up these leaves."

A murmur ripples through the crowd, who, having lost interest in the boy in the tree, grumble loudly about "another flippin' shambles" as they drift towards the town. Seeing an opportunity to promote himself, Councillor Beattie slips delicately amongst them, eagerly shaking hands, stroking dogs and kissing children – with the exception of Esther, who backs away and hides behind her mum.

Grimacing at the councillor's toadying behaviour, PC Dally strolls back to his motorcycle, flicks on his radio and makes a call to the fire service.

To Noah's shame a huge fire engine arrives, and a long ladder is extended up the side of the tree until it rests against his branch. The wheelchair is brought down first. Then Noah's humiliation is complete when a big fireman flings him over his shoulder, like a sack of potatoes, and carries him down the ladder, to the safety of the pavement. The fire chief is baffled. She takes a long, quizzical look at Noah, who is busy settling himself back into his wheelchair.

"I haven't the faintest idea how you got yourself up that

tree, my lad," she says, taking her helmet off and scratching her head as she crouches beside Noah's wheelchair. "But … well … just don't do it again, do I make myself clear?"

"I'm sorry," says Noah, defiantly, "but I had no choice. I promise I won't do it again … unless I absolutely have to, of course."

"You had better not," shouts the fire chief, over her shoulder, as she runs towards the fire engine that has been called away to put out an actual fire. "Because, next time, we might not come to your rescue."

Having satisfied himself that everyone is safe, PC Dally roars off on his motorcycle, and Noah, relieved that his protest is over, is left sitting in the shadow of the tree.

"We did it," he says, gently stroking the rough bark that had torn the skin from his arms just a few hours earlier. "We bloomin' well did it."

When the only people left are Noah and his family, his mum turns his hands over to inspect his wounded wrists. Seeing the dried bloody scratches, she lets out a heavy sigh.

"Oh, Noah, what are you like?" she says, kindly. "You always have an axe to grind."

"It's important, Mum," says Noah. "We need to stop people being so destructive."

"I want to go up the tree," Esther screeches, flinging herself to the ground in a noisy tantrum when she is refused her wish. She is still wailing and still kicking when her mum scoops her up and carries her, under one arm, towards the house.

Without exchanging one word, Noah and his dad set about picking up the discarded leaflets. They are stuffing the papers into a recycling bin when the council workmen return from their most recent tea break, and prepare to start trimming the tree.

Deciding that he had better make an appearance, Peter steps out from his hiding place behind the campervan and saunters across the road, hands stuffed into his pockets, looking as casual as he can manage.

"How on earth did you get up there in the first place?" Noah's dad is questioning him just as Peter joins them. "I expect you had something to do with it, Peter Fairchild – am I right?"

Puffing out his cheeks, Peter shakes his head and blows, saying, "Erm ... nope." He hopes that he sounds innocent.

"My lips are sealed," says Noah, pretending to zip his lips shut.

"Hmmm," says Noah's dad, arching his eyebrows to peer over the top of his glasses at Peter.

Noah is stuffing the last of the mashed-up leaflets into the bin when the workmen begin to mutter about "time getting on" and "moving the public out of the way" so that they can get to work on the tree.

Peter, Noah, and his dad decide to make their way to the house, for a much needed breakfast. Hesitating for a second, Peter turns his head, eyes fixed on Noah's branch, high in the tree. Shutting out the world for a second, he lets his eyelids close and tries to imagine the beautiful blue glow that had seemed to come to his assistance the night before. Desperately searching his memory, he is disappointed that he cannot recall the image.

"Noah, did you notice anything weird last night?" asks Peter, thinking about the electric blue light that had come to his rescue.

"Oh, yeah," says Noah, remembering Peter's strange, robotic behaviour. "What was all that about?"

"Must've been a trick of the light?" says Peter, shrugging casually, his voice falling to a whisper.

"What?" says Noah, over his shoulder, only half listening, his wheels turned in the direction of home. "Erm, yeah, whatever. Who knows?"

Chapter 3

PIGS!

Angela Omaboe is running late when she hands a tiny grey rabbit to Polly, who holds the warm little body, nervously, in her cupped hands. Angela's garden-shed-hospital has had a busy week.

"We're a bit behind," she says. "Help me feed this lot and then we can go."

"Erm, okay," says Polly, her face distorting into a frown because she can't seem to make the rabbit sit still and offer him the feeding bottle at the same time. "But we'll need to hurry, or we'll miss the wheelchair boy."

"Cheryl's due to take over soon and she's never late," says Angela, looking up from a hedgehog with an eye infection and adding, "Polly, what are you doing to that poor little rabbit?"

"Do you ever worry about leaving Cheryl here on her own?" asks Polly, distractedly, trying to wipe spilled milk formula with one hand and manage the lively little rabbit with the other. "You know, with her having ... you know?"

"Down Syndrome," says Angela, extending both hands towards Polly, reaching for the rabbit. "It's called Down Syndrome, Pol ... and just why should I be worried about that?"

"I don't know," says Polly, adding, "I just thought ..."

"Well, don't! And give me that baby before he starves

to death!" snaps Angela, snatching the rabbit from Polly's hands. "She's better at this than you are. She's never off the internet. She's like the bloomin' oracle when it comes to wildlife."

Flicking long blonde hair over her shoulders, Polly lowers her eyes, fixing them on the hungry little rabbit as it settles on Angela's lap. It eats greedily from an eye dropper, and then stretches before curling into a ball, ready to sleep. With a confidence that Polly can only watch and admire, Angela settles the rabbit into a bed box, checks on a hedgehog with a bandaged leg, and then picks up a blackbird. Her makeshift wildlife hospital has been going for months now, and she is becoming quite skilled at looking after sick little animals.

The wooden door creaks before sticking on the uneven floor until Cheryl, the volunteer nurse, kicks it open and strolls into the shed. Picking up Cheryl's scent, the animals whistle and chirrup excitedly, and Polly notices a few rainbow coloured flecks that seem to sparkle around Cheryl's perfectly styled hair, like a tinsel halo. She teases Angela.

"You really need to dust this place, Angela Omaboe," Polly says. "I can see particles floating everywhere."

"Hi Cher," says Angela, ignoring Polly's remark. "Can you take over for a while? Polly and I want to go to the skate park. There's something on today that we don't want to miss. I'll be back soon, I promise."

"It wouldn't be that blond boy with the shopping trolley by any chance," says Cheryl, checking her mauve nail polish before looking sideways at Polly, "would it?"

"No, it would not!" says Polly, her cheeks burning beetroot red. "If you must know, it's a skateboard competition, and we don't want to miss it."

She looks squarely at Angela.

"What have you been saying about me, Angela Omaboe?"

Shooting a glance at Cheryl, Angela shakes her head,

trying, without much success, to look innocent. Cheryl shrugs, pulls on a pair of latex gloves, picks up a clipboard, and flips a few papers. She scans the patient care schedules for the day.

"Yeah, whatever," she says, concentrating on the clipboard to avoid accidentally making eye contact with Polly. "Well, you'd better go then, hadn't you."

Frowning, Angela gently hands a very poorly little chaffinch to Cheryl, who coos over the bird, like a mother with a newborn infant.

"Come to mummeee, baybee," she says, gently covering the tiny body with a little square of pink fleece fabric. "I'll tuck you in for a wovewy wittle sweep."

Polly winces.

"Does she always talk to them like that?" she whispers to Angela, as they step out of the hot little shed to feel the late morning sunshine on their faces.

"I heard that," shouts Cheryl, stifling a giggle.

Polly winces again.

"Oh, come on Pol," says Angela, laughing. "We'd better get a wiggle on if we want to catch that wheelchair boy's performance. Oh and by the way, Polly Proudfoot, our hospital is spotless. You won't find any dust particles floating about in there!"

* * * * *

At the skate park, the girls head straight for Mr Brown's burger van, and take their usual place in the long queue at the side window. The battered old van reeks of grease and onions, but the girls don't mind because Mr Brown sells the best pulled pork burgers in town. Taking their food to the old Victorian fountain, the girls sit on the edge, next to a stone fish-like creature that looks as if it is gasping for air. The fountain gives Polly the creeps, but it is the best place to sit if they want to get a clear view of the skateboarding arena.

"Holy moly, Polly, this is fantastic," purrs Angela, wiping

a drip of bacon fat from her chin as they settle themselves to watch the competition.

"Hhhmf," says Polly, her mouth stuffed full of tasty pork, "delicious ... Mr Brown is amazing."

Angela digs Polly hard, in the ribs.

"There he is ... now the show really starts," she says, nodding towards the clubhouse, where Noah Fitzroy, tilted back and balanced on two wheels, is bumping his acid green sports wheelchair down the white wooden steps.

The girls watch Noah making his way to the start of the ramp, where he lowers himself onto the first step. Folding his wheelchair, he flings it up the steps ahead of himself before going up, step by step, on his bottom. At the top platform, he opens the chair and clutches the frame before effortlessly flipping himself up and onto the seat. Tightening his helmet strap, he looks down and raises both hands in a thumbs-up to his adoring fans, who whoop and cheer before they fall into an expectant silence.

Angela watches wide eyed, as the little sports wheelchair teeters on the edge of the half-pipe skateboard ramp, waiting to begin the descent. Too scared to look, Polly turns her head, prompting Angela to make fun of her.

"I don't know why you come here, Polly Proudfoot, I really don't!" she says. "You always miss everything ... are you listening to me?"

Polly is not listening. Her attention is directed towards the tall blond boy who has just entered the park, through the gate next to the clubhouse, trundling a tartan shopping trolley behind him. She can't help staring as Peter sets down his trolley, looks up at Noah on top of the ramp and points to his watch.

"Hey, Noah, I can't stay long," he shouts. "I've got to get this stuff into town before tea time."

Removing his helmet, Noah grins as he calls back.

"Okay Pete. No worries. I'll be down in no time."

Polly sighs. Angela tuts.

"He looks like a bloomin' weirdo with that trolley," she

says. "I wonder what he's got in there that's so precious he can't leave it at home."

"Maybe he's an eccentric millionaire and it's crammed full of money," says Polly, wistfully.

"Maybe it's the crown jewels," says Angela, "or maybe he's just a flippin' nutter."

Polly frowns, absentmindedly. She rather likes the look of the tall, blond boy … shopping trolley or no shopping trolley.

* * * * *

On the long walk home after the competition, romantic visions of the boy with the tartan trolley occupy Polly's imagination, and she wonders if it is possible to literally burst with happiness. Feeling that she might actually be floating on air, she turns the corner into her road and saunters up the narrow lane, towards the house. A large black van is parked in the yard and a man, wearing a blue overall and wellington boots, is speaking with her father. Her pet pigs, Ham and Rasher, are huddled behind him, their bodies pressed against the wall under the kitchen window.

"What's going on Mum?" asks Polly, pushing on the side gate, her happy thoughts popping like soap bubbles.

"POLLY! You're home early!" says her mum, hurriedly taking her aside; turning her, so that she has her back to the van. "Well … you see, dear, the pigs have grown too big for us to keep, and so, they're … erm … going to live on a farm … where they will be happier."

"But they're happy here," says Polly, craning her neck to see what is happening behind her. "They're my pets."

Her mum says nothing.

"I don't understand, Mum," Polly continues, a knot forming in her stomach, making her feel sick as confusion turns to fear. "Why are you saying that they have to go?"

On her father's command, Ham and Rasher walk obediently up a metal ramp and disappear into the darkness of the van. Almost immediately their huge faces reappear with flat round snouts pressing through the bars. Their bewildered eyes are fixed on Polly, pleading with her to help them. She desperately wants to protect them, as she has done ever since they were tiny piglets, but her mother's uncompromising outstretched hand will not allow it.

"Mum … please … I'm begging you … don't do this," says Polly.

"Oh, grow up, Polly!" snaps her mum. "They were supposed to be micro pigs. Look at them – they're huge! We can't possibly keep them. We need to let them go, and that's the end of it."

Utterly powerless, Polly bursts into tears.

The man takes a wad of banknotes from his pocket and counts some money into her dad's outstretched hand. Sniffing deeply, he coughs and spits before slamming the back doors shut and then clambering into the front. Shuddering into life, the van finally drives away, with the beloved pigs, squealing, in the back.

"But they're happy *here*." is all that Polly can whisper, as she watches the van disappear around the corner, swathed in a choking grey mist that leaves a slowly evaporating trail in its wake. Pressing a tissue to her face, Polly's mother turns on her heel and stalks across the yard. Looking straight ahead, she steps through the back door and is immediately swallowed by the dark old house.

"I'm really sorry, Polly," says her dad, with his back to her, his stride faltering momentarily before he decides to follow his wife.

The pigs are gone and, suddenly, Polly's world makes no sense. Everything is turned upside down, and her heart is wrenched apart. In a daze, she looks around the pig field. It seems huge. The pig shed is empty, and everywhere is eerily quiet. Exhausted and defeated, she slumps onto the big boulder by the gate and she weeps until she aches.

* * * * *

Hours later, her bottom feeling cold against the stone, Polly is still sitting with her chin in her hands. She is startled when, leaning heavily on her walking stick, old Mrs Jones limps up the lane accompanied by Benjamin, her unruly and very untidy mongrel terrier.

"Whatever is the matter, Polly," asks the old lady, bending over her stick and struggling to attach Benjamin's lead to his harness. "Has something happened?"

Looking up through red, tear-filled eyes, Polly swallows to clear the lump in her throat, and blows her nose on a corner of her skirt, before she can tell Mrs Jones what has happened.

"My pigs have been taken to live on a farm because they grew too big," she says, her voice breaking like hiccups. "And I can't understand how my dad could have sent them away. I don't know what to do, Mrs Jones."

"Hmmm …" the old woman purses her lips and her eyebrows rise, furrowing her forehead as she looks Polly straight in the eye. "And do you believe that, my dear?"

"What?" says Polly, meeting Mrs Jones' tough, steely stare.

"Polly, dear," says Mrs Jones, with absolute clarity, "your pigs haven't gone to any farm; they've been taken to the abattoir, to be killed, and turned into pork chops and sausages, so that people can eat them."

"Eat them?" says Polly "Did you say … eat them? NO WAY!"

Leaving her words hanging in the air, Polly springs to her feet and, before she can take another breath, is racing towards the house, calling a quick, "Oh, thanks," over her shoulder.

"You are welcome, my dear," Mrs Jones calls after her, in a duet with Benjamin, who, having jumped onto the boulder, is barking as loud as he can. "I hope you can save them."

Colliding with the back door, Polly kicks it aside as she bursts into the house, yelling to her parents at the top of her voice. "MUM! DAD! You sent my pigs to be killed?" She runs from room to room. "You sent them to die. You lied to me. How could you do that?"

Her mum and dad are sitting at the battered old kitchen table. They are talking in low, husky voices.

"I think we've made a terrible mistake," her dad is saying. He leans on the table and it wobbles under his weight, spilling water from his glass. Half-heartedly mopping the liquid with an old cotton tea towel, her mum is nodding wearily when she notices Polly glowering at them from the doorway, both fists firmly planted on her hips.

"Right," says her dad. "We need to get them back. Come on."

Grabbing the keys to his van, he hurries outside and jumps into the driver's seat. Polly and her mum jump in next to him, and, before they can pull the door closed, the van is speeding away, towards the abattoir.

The creaky old van barely stays upright as it shoots along the country roads with the back wheels swinging round bends, the brakes squealing to a halt at every crossroads. They are waiting at a red traffic light when PC Dally pulls up alongside them, on his motorcycle. Leaning over to say hello, the young policeman frowns when he sees Polly's distress. His frown deepens when she explains the reason why she is crying.

"I see …," he says, "… right then, you'd better hurry."

Flicking on the light at the back of his motorcycle, PC Dally speeds ahead of the van. Stopping the traffic, he waves the family straight through every junction, until they arrive at their dreadful destination. The abattoir is protected by a set of enormous wrought iron gates, with the words 'JDC Suppliers of Fine Meats' embedded in a black metal archway that spans the entrance. The van wheels crunch loudly onto a large gravel car park, but Polly can still hear the desperate cries of the condemned animals. She is shocked to her very core.

"This is horrible," she thinks, "this is really, really horrible."

Two huge steel doors start to move and creak when the head of a worker juts out, scanning left and right he checks the yard before he locks up for the night.

"We're late," she screams, in a panic, her fingers frantically feeling for the seatbelt release. "We're too late! My pigs are in there. I'm going in. Let me go, Mum! LET … ME … GO!"

"Polly, stop … look!" says her mum, holding her around the waist.

She stops struggling long enough to see her dad and PC Dally running into the abattoir. Flinging her seat belt aside, Polly leaps from the van and, with long powerful strides, hares after them. She just manages to squeeze her body through the narrow gap as the solid metal doors clunk shut, behind her.

Inside the dimly lit building, the air is foul and suffocating. Almost retching at the smell, the policeman, Polly, and her dad pick their way along a maze of cluttered corridors, to a gloomy office marked, 'JD Cleaver: Proprietor.' Standing silently in the doorway, they watch Mr Cleaver for a moment. Hunched over his desk, like a garden gargoyle, he is counting an enormous wad of money, his long bony fingers lovingly caressing each banknote, as if it was somehow alive.

He doesn't bother to look up.

"We're closed!" he barks, scaring Polly so much that she shrinks back, behind her dad. "Get out!"

"I want my pigs back, Mr Cleaver," says Polly's dad, shooting a sideways glance at PC Dally.

"Oh, do you now," says Mr Cleaver, half smiling. "You'll get them back all right – in a freezer bag."

The slaughter man breaks into a spine-chilling laugh.

Polly shudders.

"I want them back alive," says her dad, carefully.

"Alive?" says Mr Cleaver, his head snapping up, and his sharp close-set eyes fixing on Polly's dad. "Well … it'll cost you."

"I still have your money here … see," says Polly's dad, holding the crumpled notes in his outstretched hand. "You can have it all back."

"Oh, that won't be enough," says Mr Cleaver, a thin crooked smile contorting his bony face. "Not nearly enough. That is, if you want them back … alive."

"How much do you want?"

"Double it and you can have them back," says Mr Cleaver, adding, "Life is so unfair … isn't it, Mr Proudfoot?"

Petrified that her father will not agree to pay so much, Polly is convinced that her pigs will never get out of the abattoir alive. Her body starts to tremble, until she is shaking so much that she can feel her teeth chattering. PC Dally puts a reassuring hand on her shoulder and winks before raising his eyebrows as he looks sideways at her dad.

Mr Proudfoot takes in a long, deep, steadying breath.

"How do I know they are still alive?" he asks, cautiously.

"You don't think I have time to collect them and kill them on the same day, do you, Mr Proudfoot?" says Mr Cleaver. "I'm far too busy for that."

"Okay. Let me see them, and I'll pay whatever you want," says Polly's dad.

"Is that a firm deal?" asks Mr Cleaver.

"Deal," says Polly's dad, "… and you have my word."

"Very well then," says Mr Cleaver, putting his money box into a desk drawer, which he is careful to lock before picking up a ring of enormous keys and heaving himself up from his desk. "Follow me."

Jangling his keys like a jailer, Mr Cleaver leads them down a passageway so narrow that PC Dally's shoulders knock against the stone walls on either side. They are approaching the holding pens when Polly recognises two flat snouts pushing through a set of bars. At the first sniff of Polly's familiar scent, Ham and Rasher start to squeal with excitement. Her heart racing, Polly has to stop herself from running to her pigs, because the transaction is not completed and Mr Cleaver could easily change his mind and kill the pigs anyway.

"Pay up," says Mr Cleaver, "or these ugly brutes get the chop first thing tomorrow morning."

"Let's go to your office and get on with it," says Polly's dad.

PC Dally and Polly stay behind with the stockman, to oversee Ham and Rasher's release, whilst her dad follows Mr Cleaver back to his office to make the payment.

They regroup at the abattoir doors.

"You must be mad," Mr Cleaver calls after them, as they walk between the metal doors with Ham and Rasher trotting behind them. "They're only porkers. They're for butchering. Nothing else. Well, they're your problem now."

"Right!" says PC Dally, his body stiffening as he turns on his heel, and stalks back towards the building. "Now that's done, I have to inform you, Mr Cleaver, that I will be asking the authorities for a full inspection of this building, first thing tomorrow morning, and regular checks after that ... let's say ... twice a week."

"But ... that's harassment," says Mr Cleaver, his hands folding into tight bony fists.

PC Dally forces a smile and, through gritted teeth, says, "Life is so unfair ... isn't it, Mr Cleaver?"

It is late when they trudge out of the abattoir, into the damp grey evening. Everybody is exhausted but they are happy that the pigs have been saved.

"Well done, young Polly," says PC Dally, just before he closes the visor on his helmet. "Those are two very lucky animals you've got there."

The broad-shouldered policeman straddles his motorcycle, kicks the starter, and, like a fairytale knight on his horse, raises a gauntleted hand in a salute, as the engine roar fades and he disappears into the distance. After quite a few turns of the engine, Mr Proudfoot's rusty old van splutters into life, and, as they make their way home, Polly, who is still very angry, decides to challenge her parents.

"How could you have put Ham and Rash ... the pigs ... in such danger?" she demands. "I can't believe that you did that to them."

"Now just you wait a minute, young lady," says her dad, crossly. "Before you start throwing accusations about. You eat meat, don't you? Where the hell did you think it came from?"

"Oh … well … I don't know," says Polly. "I … I hadn't thought about it before."

"Well, you'd better start thinking about it, madam, before you blame us," snaps her dad, almost losing control of his steering wheel.

"I'm sorry … I …" says Polly, biting hard on her trembling lip, tears gathering around her eyes.

"So, anyway," says Mrs Proudfoot, smiling and putting a comforting hand on Polly's lap, "what do we do now?"

"We go veggie," says her dad. "Give it a try, you know? See how we get on with it. What do you think, Polly?"

"Yeah, we could," says Polly, who knows exactly what she wants to do, but says nothing, because first she needs to get some serious advice.

✳   ✳   ✳   ✳   ✳

Now that they are standing outside Mrs Jones' neat little cottage, Polly and Angela are feeling nervous. It had seemed like a great idea when they discussed it at the skateboard park, but now that they are waiting for the old lady to answer, Polly hasn't a clue how she will broach the subject.

Benjamin's nails click as he jumps about in the hall, barking frantically, whilst Mrs Jones slides a bolt, releases a chain, turns a key in the lock, and then opens the door.

"Out of the way, Benjami… oh, hello, Polly," she says, nudging the excited little dog with her stick before rubbing a swollen arthritic knee. "What a surprise. Is everything all right?"

"Yes, thank you," says Polly. "I just wanted to … to … erm."

"Is something bothering you, my dear?" asks Mrs Jones, glancing down at Angela, who is on her knees stroking the lively little dog.

"Yes," is all that Polly can think of saying.

"Come on in, girls," says Mrs Jones. "I was just going to have some tea."

With Benjamin doing his utmost to trip everyone up, the girls follow Mrs Jones into a tiny lounge, and thread, single file, around an enormous flowery patterned sofa. Then the old lady leads them through a busy little kitchen that opens into an equally cramped, over-furnished conservatory. Crystals hang in every window, casting rainbows that dance around the girls as Mrs Jones invites them to take a seat. Then she disappears into the kitchen where she overfills a wooden tray with a mismatch of chipped crockery, cakes, juice, and a pot of tea. Finally the three of them sit around a small cast iron bistro table.

"We saved the pigs," says Polly, proudly.

"Yes," says Mrs Jones. "I heard about that."

"I wanted to thank you for telling me the truth," says Polly.

"You are welcome, my dear," says Mrs Jones. "Though, to be honest Polly, I was surprised that you hadn't worked it out for yourself."

"I ... I just didn't think about things like that before," says Polly, lowering her eyes and swiping a finger across her lashes.

"Anyway," continues Mrs Jones, kindly, "it was your quick action that saved them, and that's the main thing."

"And PC Dally," says Polly. "We really couldn't have done it without him. He was brilliant."

"Yes, well, he is vegan," says Mrs Jones, cutting a slice of cake and handing it to Polly, on a faded willow pattern plate.

"Really?" says Angela, reaching across the table for a scone, before helping herself to the pot of jam. "Vegan, eh ... I never knew that."

"We are very ordinary people," says Mrs Jones, dripping some tea onto her skirt. "Oh drat, I shall have to wash that now ... what was I saying ... oh, yes ... and there are a lot of us about, you know."

"Well, I'm glad my family no longer eats animals," says Polly.

"Mine too," says Angela, spitting out scone crumbs that roll down her t-shirt towards Benjamin, who is waiting to eat them the second they hit the floor.

"We wish everyone would stop," continues Polly, grimacing at Angela's lack of table manners, "and we want to do something, don't we Angela? Tell people, start a campaign … you know."

Mrs Jones nods, thoughtfully.

"Oh, I felt exactly the same when I was your age," she says. "But you can't tell people what to do, girls. You can only inform them, and many will disagree with you."

Delicately settling her cup on the saucer, Mrs Jones leans forward, and taps a neatly trimmed fingernail on the metal table.

"A lot of people make a lot of money from animals," she says, her voice low and serious, "and they won't like you meddling with their sales. Could you girls cope with them? You will need to summon all of your courage. Do you think you can do that?"

"Of course," says Angela, confidently. "We can manage that. We're not frightened of them, are we, Pol?"

"Erm … no … I suppose not," says Polly, uncertainly, though she knows in her heart that they really have no choice in the matter, because they are meant to do this. She can feel it. It is their job.

* * * * *

Several hours and several arguments later, Polly and Angela finally manage to agree on a design for their campaign leaflets.

Deciding to call their cause 'Veggie' they print the leaflets on pink paper: Polly's favourite colour. When the girls are satisfied with their efforts, they each put a bundle of leaflets into their school rucksack.

"We can pass these flyers around the school dining hall

and then see what happens," says Angela, confidently. "This is gonna be brilliant, Pol!"

But, anxious about drawing attention to themselves, the girls keep the leaflets hidden in their rucksacks, and it is two full weeks before they can pluck up enough courage to distribute them. They finally settle on a busy Friday lunchtime, when the crowded little dining hall is bustling with rattling cutlery and crashing dishes. Swathed in steam from the hot food counter, the dinner ladies' faces glisten with sweat, as they run around the stainless steel kitchen, trying to serve lunch to an entire hungry school.

Standing in a corner by the door, Polly and Angela watch the children happily tucking into burgers, sausages and pies, completely unaware of what they are actually eating. Nudging Polly in the ribs, Angela flicks her bundle of veggie leaflets, her face breaking into a wide grin as she tilts her head towards the diners.

"Ready?" she whispers.

Polly is nodding when, quite suddenly, her confidence dissolves and her legs begin to tremble as Mrs Jones' words ring in her ears. Could she really land in serious trouble for what she is about to do? What will her parents say? Shaking her head, Polly turns to look at Angela, deciding to tell her that she can't go thought with it. She has changed her mind.

"Angela, I don't …"

In the corner by the drinks machine, a tower of golden sunlight begins to form: dancing and flickering, until it sends out long shining rays, like a summer sunrise. It is the clearest, purest gold that Polly has ever seen and she cannot summon the strength to look away. The hubbub of the dining room fades into the distance as Polly gazes, transfixed, unable to break the connection. Sheer power fires straight into her body like a rush of electricity, energising and strengthening her, until a voice as delicate as tinkling crystal, fills her head.

"Polly, don't be afraid. You must go forward … this is your job."

Her heart thuds, skipping beats and pounding in her chest as she feels herself growing in confidence, feels, somehow, invincible. Finally tearing her eyes away from the angel-light Polly turns her gaze back to Angela.

"Are you ready, Angela?" she asks, softly.

"Too right I am," says Angela, in her usual fearless way. "Come on, Polly: let's get this done ... once and for all."

The girls take the first faltering step, and, before they know it, they are walking about the jam-packed little dining hall, deftly weaving between the Formica tables. As quickly as they can, and without saying a single word, they place a leaflet beside each of the diners until, less than fifteen minutes later, every child in the hall is looking at a pink 'Veggie' flyer. The mysterious tower of golden sunlight has disappeared and the corner has returned to darkness, but Polly and Angela feel elated, now that their campaign is definitely under way.

"YES!" shrieks Polly, punching her fist high into the air.

*　*　*　*　*

In the weeks that follow, the girls dutifully answer relentless questions and lead endless discussions, day after day, in the playground. But no one seems to understand their message. No one is really interested in what they have to say.

Angela is first to bring it up.

"We need to face the facts, Pol," she says. "It's a disaster; we've failed, big time."

"But we can't fail, Angela," says Polly. "It's too important."

"Pol, nobody is interested," says Angela, straightforwardly. "I vote we give up. I know how you feel, but I ..."

"No! You don't know how I feel," says Polly, interrupting her. "You didn't see what I saw in that awful place."

"I'm sorry, Polly," says Angela, laying her hand on Polly's shoulder, "but it really is over."

Abruptly shrugging Angela's hand away, Polly sighs, her thoughts turning to the golden angel-light that had encouraged her to start the campaign in the first place. Why would it do that to her? It seems so cruel to get her hopes up, only to have them crushed. Why didn't it help her? Then an unusual request comes from a completely unexpected source.

Henry Spratt is exceptionally small for his age, the smallest boy in his year. Being the youngest of three boys, his hand-me-down clothes are always just a little on the big side, emphasising his thin little body and seemingly oversized head. But whatever Henry lacks in physical stature, he makes up for with an enormous personality, and he is popular with pretty much everybody at school.

"Oi, Polly," Henry calls across the playground, raising an arm so thin that the elbow sticks out like a ping pong ball. "Can I come and see your pigs?"

"Hey, Henry," says Polly, "are you thinking of going vegetarian?"

"Dunno … maybe … maybe not," says Henry, spitting through the plastic brace on his oversized teeth. "I'll let you know when I've made up my mind. So, can I come then … or what?"

"Sure," says Polly, hopefully. "You can come on Saturday if you like, and bring someone along with you, if you want."

"Yeah," says Henry, "I might."

It is exactly nine o'clock on Saturday morning when Polly, who has been taken at her word, looks out of the kitchen window to see Henry, leading a battalion of schoolchildren, that he refers to as "a few of my mates," up the lane towards her house. Before Polly can get a chance to exchange her slippers for wellingtons, two dozen children swarm through the gate and congregate in the yard. Then, like a flock of starlings, the children move as one body. Chattering and laughing, they swoop around the yard, out to the field and into the pig shed, with Polly, her mum and Mrs Jones running around: herding them like sheep. Ending up in the kitchen, the children devour every morsel of Mrs Jones' veggie snacks and tasters. Then, as quickly as they had arrived, they pour out of the gate and disappear down the lane amid calls of "thanks," and "brilliant," and "fantastic."

Looking back from the front of the troop and waving his thin hand in the air, Henry shouts, "Cheers Polly, that was great. See you at school on Monday."

"Are you going veggie?" shouts Polly.

"Dunno … maybe … probably," says Henry, leaving an exhausted and very grateful Polly rushing to her phone to call Angela.

Henry and his mates tell everyone about their visit to Polly's pigs, and it is not long before children start asking their parents if they can try some vegetarian food at home. A few of the braver children even refuse the meaty school lunches. But, just as Mrs Jones had predicted, many of them make fun of the girls, and they say that they would never give up eating animals. Mandy Skinner, the butcher's daughter, is one of them. She tells her dad about the 'Veggie' campaign at school.

"They can't do that!" snarls the butcher, wiping a bloody hand on his striped apron, before reaching for the sawdust covered telephone. "I'm not standing for it. Those interfering little pests have got to be stopped!"

The butcher calls Mr Cleaver, the slaughter man, who calls Mr McSwiney, the farmer, who calls Mr Brown, the burger man, who calls Miss Carver, the delicatessen lady. The five tradespeople meet. They talk, compare notes, and are horrified when they realise that every one of them has had a drop in sales. Furious about Polly and Angela's campaign, they march into the school, demanding that the girls be stopped … with immediate effect.

✳ ✳ ✳ ✳ ✳

Class 2B is enduring a particularly boring history lesson when Angela, who is gazing out of the window, notices the five shopkeepers as they barge through the school gates, stalk across the playground, and crash through the swing doors into the school. Polly is struggling to stay awake. Both of her elbows are on the desk, her chin is supported in cupped hands, and her eyelids are desperately trying to close. She hardly notices Mrs Baker, the school secretary, coming into the classroom and whispering into the teacher's ear.

Ms Thompson, whose quiet monotone voice always sends the children to sleep, scans the class, looking for the girls, and then, speaking unusually loudly, says, "Polly! Angela! Please go with Mrs Baker to the head teacher's office. Quickly now!"

Startled from their daydreams, the girls leap to their feet, push their chairs out of the way and scramble, noisily, from behind their desks. Walking briskly out of the class, they fall into line, behind the secretary. Looking sideways at Polly, Angela frowns and tries to find out what is wrong.

"What's happened, Mrs Baker?" she asks. "Is there some sort of trouble?"

But the skittish little secretary refuses to say a word and the girls follow her in complete silence, along the stuffy, window-lined corridor. They are approaching the head teacher's office when a sudden wave of fear flips Polly's stomach and she casts a glance towards Angela, whose head is up, defiant as usual. Polly is filled with admiration for her brave friend, though she doesn't share her confidence.

Mrs Salmon, the head teacher, red faced, and so upset that her orange lipstick has run into the creases around her mouth, comes out to meet them in the corridor. Straight-backed, her sensible brogues squeaking against the polished floor, Mrs Salmon strides purposefully, towards the girls.

"I hear that you two have been handing out leaflets around this school," she says in a loud voice, her usual poise abandoning her. "Is that … hmm, correct?"

"Yes, Mrs Salmon," says Polly, tilting her head to look past the teacher at the five complainers, who are standing in a huddle, in the office. When they spot Polly and Angela, the group erupts like an angry volcano.

"There's the little ..." cries the butcher, pointing at Polly, his voice echoing through the whole school.

"I'll flaming well pulverise those two," screams Mr Cleaver, waving his arm through the air as if wielding an imaginary weapon.

"Not if I get them first," growls Farmer McSwiney, his hands balled into two hard fists.

"Oh, really, girls ... I mean ... well ... how could you!" says the delicatessen lady, delicately patting her perfectly coiffured hair.

"Let me get my hands on them," shouts the burger man, elbowing Miss Carver aside, then adding, "wait a minute, those two were my best customers."

Seeming to merge into one giant angry monster made entirely of legs, heads and fists, the tradespeople advance towards the girls. Running for the door, Mrs Salmon is just in time to pull it shut, and the monster crashes into it, banging and shouting from the inside.

As an afterthought, she shoves Mrs Baker into the room saying, "Calm them down will you, there's a dear," before closing the door again and turning her attention to the girls.

"They've called the police, Angela," she says. "What on earth have you two been up to?"

The colour drains from Polly's face and, convinced that she is going to be sick, she swallows back some saliva that burns the back of her throat.

"The police?" she says, both hands shooting up to push her fringe over the top of her head. "It's all my fault, Mrs Salmon. I asked Angela to help me. I'm to blame. Oh no ... my mum and dad will go ape."

"Well?" demands Mrs Salmon, looking at Angela. "I'm waiting."

"We both did it," says Angela, without flinching. "And I would do it again, because it's important. I would – wouldn't I, Pol?"

In a flurry of anxiety and fear, words tumble out of Polly's mouth as she tries to explain how her pet pigs were saved, that she has been inside an abattoir, and that she just wants to save other animals from going there.

"That can't be wrong, now can it, Mrs Salmon?" asks Angela.

Polly's legs feel like jelly, as if her knees are melting away.

"Can it?" she says, in a whisper, trying desperately not to cry.

"No, Polly, it is not wrong," says Mrs Salmon, unusually kindly, "but, if you want to run a campaign in this school, you must let the staff know what you are doing."

"I'm sorry, Mrs Salmon," says Polly.

"We didn't think to …" says Angela.

"Besides," the head teacher continues, "I might be able to help you girls, but first we need to deal with this rabble in my office. Just exactly how did you save these pigs of yours?"

Before Polly can answer Mrs Salmon's question, a deep voice booms from the other end of the corridor.

"They were saved, in the nick of time, by a very brave young lady," says PC Dally.

PC Dally had been sent to investigate.

Polly almost laughs with relief.

"Now then," says the policeman, winking at Polly, "what's the story here?"

Mrs Salmon explains the situation for PC Dally, who frowns.

"So you couldn't let it rest, then, eh, young Polly?" he says, cocking his head to one side.

"I couldn't sit back and do nothing," says Polly. "I didn't mean to cause any trouble. I just want people to stop being so cruel."

Uncontrollable tears well in Polly's eyes, spilling down her cheeks. She begins to wobble until her knees give way, and she slumps, sobbing, to the floor. Immediately, Angela is sitting at her side, arms flung around her friend, in a reassuring hug. PC Dally and Mrs Salmon exchange a brief look of sympathy for the girls. Then they look at the office door.

"Oh, my goodness, I forgot about Mrs Baker! They'll have eaten her alive," says Mrs Salmon, rushing off and bringing the smile back to Polly's face.

Opening the office door, Mrs Salmon finds Mrs Baker crouched behind a filing cabinet, hiding from the angry mob that is now one seething mass. It surges forward, intent on grabbing the girls, until it notices the policeman standing in the corridor. The mass hesitates, growls a little and then, gradually, morphs back into the five furious business people.

The slaughter man speaks first.

"Are you here to arrest these little brats?" he demands.

"And why would I do that?" asks PC Dally, calmly.

"They're ruining our businesses. Lock 'em up," shouts the butcher.

"They're criminals. Get them behind bars," says Farmer McSwiney.

PC Dally sighs.

"They are only standing up for their beliefs, and they have a right to do that," he says, adding, "I won't be locking anybody up – unless you keep harassing these young ladies: then I might lock you up."

Gasping in unison, the rabble takes a step back. All except Miss Carver, the delicatessen lady, who steps delicately forward, towards the young policeman.

"Oh, you are so right, Constable Dally," she says, breathlessly patting a hand to her chest. "We must all have the right to express our beliefs."

The mob glares at her, but Miss Carver is looking longingly at the policeman, and fluttering her false eyelashes. Angela can't help sniggering as PC Dally and Miss Carver gaze at each other amid the chaos.

"Constable Dally! They're leaving!" snaps Mrs Salmon, trying, with little success, to uphold her authority in the school, and adding, "Are you going to follow your friends, Miss Carver? MISS CARVER!"

"Hmmm ... what? Oh ... yes ... goodbye, Constable Dally," says Miss Carver, as she floats out of the door on a cloud of lilac chiffon and overpowering perfume. "À bientôt."

Shaking her head, Mrs Salmon looks up at the ceiling and sighs.

"Now, Constable," she asks, turning her attention to PC Dally. "What happens next?"

The love-struck policeman says nothing. He is staring, open-mouthed, at the door, so utterly enchanted that his eyes have completely glazed over.

"CONSTABLE DALLY!" shouts Mrs Salmon, who is clearly getting fed up with the whole affair.

"Eh, what, oh, er, yes, um," says PC Dally.

Polly and Angela exchange a secret look and start to giggle.

"Well, nothing is going to happen …" says the policeman, distractedly. " Err, would you excuse me, please. I just need to, erm …" and without turning back, he rushes out of the door to catch up with his new love, calling, "Carry on, girls, carry on."

In the silence that is left behind, Polly and Angela find themselves standing in the polished school corridor, face to face with Mrs Salmon.

"You said you might be able to help us," says Angela, bravely.

"I most certainly did, Miss Omaboe," says Mrs Salmon. "Come into my office, girls. We need to have a talk with the cook."

On Mrs Salmon's orders, Polly and Angela sit quietly, on old worn chairs, in front of her old worn desk, whilst she speaks into a very modern telephone.

"Ask Mrs Pottage to come to my office please," she says to the secretary, before replacing the receiver, replenishing her orange lipstick and pursing her lips in the ever-present make-up mirror. When she has finished admiring her reflection, Mrs Salmon looks over her desk at Polly and Angela.

"Now! I'm thinking that we might offer a vegetarian school lunch option," she says, "but only if we can still provide healthy, balanced meals. How does that sound?"

Dumbstruck, Polly and Angela can only look at each other.

They are nodding excitedly when Mrs Pottage, the school cook, scuttles into the office. She is wringing her hands.

"Yes, Head Teacher?" she says, smoothing back her hair and tidying her apron, her voice faltering. "You sent for me, Head Teacher?"

When Mrs Salmon suggests a vegetarian menu option, Mrs Pottage sways and leans against the bookshelf, as if she might pass out.

"What! I can't do that, Head Teacher," she wails, frowning and shifting from foot to foot, tugging at her apron. "A basic cook, that's me. Meat and two veg is what I do. It's traditional."

"It's old fashioned!" says Mrs Salmon. "And we are going to change the menu. Now, are you with me or are you not, Mrs Pottage?"

"Of course, Head Teacher," says Mrs Pottage, flashing a resentful look at Polly and Angela. "If you say so Head Teacher, but what do I know about vegetarian food? Nothing, that's what! I mean, how am I supposed to … ?"

Angela nudges Polly's side, raises her eyebrows and inclines her head towards the adults.

"What? Oh yes – I know someone who could help you with that," says Polly, interrupting the cook to tell them about old Mrs Jones.

"Well," says Mrs Pottage, reluctantly, "if she would help me, I'll see what I can do. If that's all right with you, Head Teacher."

Standing up, Mrs Salmon pushes her chair out of the way, and sucks in a breath so deep that her chest expands and her string of pearls rolls off to one side.

"That's settled then. Now," she says, slapping her hands together, "everyone back to work! I have a school to run."

Mrs Jones agrees to help Mrs Pottage and, to everyone's surprise, the two cooks get on extremely well, filling the dining hall with hoots of laughter, as they share recipes and stories. Their enjoyment rubs off on the children, most of whom are genuinely keen to try the new vegetarian meals. Mandy Skinner complains that she hates the new food and she always brings the fattiest, meatiest, packed lunch. But nobody says anything because it is her choice.

The local newspaper hears about Polly and Angela's successful 'Veggie' campaign and a reporter comes to the house to take photographs of the pigs for the front page.

"Now lots of people will know about our campaign," says Angela, filled with pride. "Life doesn't get any better than this."

"Yes … it does," says Polly, smiling as she hands Angela an invitation card that reads:

> *PC Eustace Dally and Miss Euphemia Carver would like to invite you to join them at their wedding.*

The local community hall is crammed full of tables, decorated with white ribbons and multi-coloured flower arrangements, for the most popular wedding reception of the year. Wearing a huge wedding gown, the new Mrs Dally swishes from table to table, like a taffeta butterfly, whilst her guests attempt to dance to a cheesy out-of-tune wedding band. Angela, angry that her mum has forced her to wear a girly dress for the occasion, is less than kind about the glowing bride.

"She looks like a melting blancmange in that thing," she whispers to Polly, who can't stop laughing.

After the wedding, alone in Polly's garden, the two girls lean on the wooden gate, watching the pigs amble about, looking content to be in their big muddy field.

"Do you think Ham and Rasher know how close they came to a horrible death?" asks Angela.

"You mean Dusty and Grubby," says Polly. "I changed their names, Angela. How on earth could I have thought it was funny to call them Ham and Rasher. I feel so ashamed."

"Hmm, do you think they know what you did for them?" asks Angela.

"I honestly don't know," says Polly. "Thanks for helping me with the Veggie campaign, Angela. I couldn't have done it without you."

"Polly," says Angela, hesitantly, "just before we started our campaign – did you see that gold light thing in the corner of the dining hall?"

"Oh … yeah," says Polly, avoiding Angela's eyes. "I meant to ask you about that. It was weird. What do you think it was?"

"I don't know," says Angela, truthfully. "A reflection from the drinks machine maybe."

"Yeah," says Polly, untruthfully. "You're probably right."

Looking straight ahead, and not at each other, the girls consider this, until Angela breaks the silence.

"Anyway," she says, "your pigs had a lot of people on their side, Polly. People do care, you know. Well, some people do. The smart ones."

"Does that make us the smart ones?" asks Polly.

Angela laughs.

"Too bloomin' right!" she says.

Chapter 4

MEETINGS WITH AN OUTSIDER

According to himself, Joshua Beadle's rightful place is sitting amongst the powerful politicians in the House of Commons. It is his right. His destiny. This morning, Josh is feeling particularly important as he stands up, between the green leather benches, to challenge the Prime Minister about some important matter or other.

"Mister Speaker, Honourable Gentlemen and Ladies, of course. Ha. Ha. I have something very important that I would like to say …" Josh is declaring his intention, when a voice cries out:

"GET OUT OF THE WAY, EINSTEIN!"

His mother's ear splitting screech and the cat's grumpy yowl jolt him awake, shattering his dream and catapulting him straight back to reality. They always blame each other. Einstein complains when Mrs Beadle trips over him and she complains that the cat gets under her feet. Josh tries to ignore the racket. Rolling onto one side, he draws his knees to his chest, curls his body into a comfortable ball and slips the soft, warm duvet over his head. For a moment he thinks about putting his fingers in his ears, but he is too tired, and much too cosy, to be bothered.

"JOSHUA BEADLE," his mum is rapping on the bedroom door and she is shouting. "You'll be late for school. GET UP!"

Battling the urge to drift back to his wonderful dream, Josh flips a corner of the duvet, opens one bleary eye and surveys his familiar surroundings. A plump cartoon woman with an elongated sort of poodle sitting at her side, smiles down at him from the poster above his desk. The woman is carrying an oversized placard that declares, in thick black letters, "Your Vote is Your Voice" and she is the first thing that Josh sees, every morning when he opens his eyes. Gazing up at the drawing, he half smiles back until he notices the rain pouring down the window and splashing into a puddle on the outside ledge. Roused from its sleep, his foggy brain takes a moment to wake up, gradually clearing until he remembers what day it is.

"Oh no," he groans, looking despondently at the weather, "now the coach will be all steamed up … oh, no, no, no!"

It is the morning of a school trip that Josh has been dreading for weeks, because the thought of spending half a day crammed into a bus filled with noisy schoolchildren, really depresses him. Then there's the destination. It is his worst nightmare.

Dragging himself out of bed, he flinches in pain when his left foot lands on the upturned three pin plug from his phone charger. Josh, who does not have a superstitious bone in his body, nevertheless takes it as an omen that his day can only get much, much worse.

"Why are they making us go on this awful trip, Dad?" he asks, his slippers shuffling into the cool, window lined, little dining room, for breakfast. "I really, really don't want to do this."

"It's a government directive, Josh, you know that," says his dad, slurping an enormous mug of black coffee and adding, "We've already discussed this. The letter said that everybody must attend, so you have to go."

"But I'll have to spend time on a school bus … with all the little kids in my class," says Josh.

"They're the same age as you, son," says his dad, patiently. "Can't you just try to get along with them for one day?"

"But they're so childish, Dad," whines Josh. "And it's a farm. It's disgusting."

His dad nods and sinks his teeth into a thick slice of toast, so full of Mrs Beadle's homemade raspberry jam that it drips down his chin and lands on the glass table top, sticking to it like a blob of thick red glue.

"All the same," he says distractedly, licking jam from his fingers and craning his neck to look for the box of tissues, "you have to go."

"Well, I'll try to get the seat by the bus driver," says Josh, who is feeling utterly fed up. "It's my only hope."

The children at school make it crystal clear that they think Josh is annoying, and everyone tells him to his face that he is boring. He is always last choice for team games, which means that he must face utter humiliation at every gym lesson. It doesn't help that Sergeant Pikestaff, the gym teacher, is an ex-army man who ridicules anyone with a lack of physical prowess. Punishing Pike, as he is better known, seems to go out of his way to let everyone know that he thinks Josh is an overweight weakling.

Reading helps a bit, and Josh's face is always buried in some book or other because he really believes that information equals power. He tries not to worry too much about what other people think of him, but nobody ever wants his company and, if he is honest about it, Josh never seems to want theirs.

Today, however, he has no choice in the matter. He has to go and, according to his dad, that is that!

* * * * *

Settling himself into the seat at the front of the bus, Josh takes *The History of Politics* out of his school rucksack, opens it at the page with the turned down corner, adjusts his glasses, and tries to read. Before long, an assortment of missiles is flying all over the bus, and a pink heart shaped rubber, thrown from the back, bounces from Josh's head to the floor before disappearing under the seat. He ignores it. The next object to make contact is a half chewed sausage roll, followed by a yellow plastic straw.

"Do you mind," snaps Josh. "Some of us are trying to read."

"Oh, lighten up, fatty," shouts a voice from the back seats.

The whole bus erupts into howls of laughter and, as usual, it is at Josh's expense.

"Erm … now children … settle down, please," whimpers Mr Brown, the timid little teacher, branded 'Beigey Brown' by the pupils, who is supposed to be in charge of the bus.

But it is the rowdy, out of tune singing that irritates Josh so much that he closes his book, slides it back into his school bag, and gazes out of the rainy steamed up window until the bus bumps up a track that seems to have more potholes than road. As much as he has been dreading the destination, Josh is grateful that the bus has arrived, because his self-control is rapidly burning out, and the last thing he wants to do is cry in front of THEM.

Turning his back to the children, Josh rests his forehead against the window, and his gaze drifts towards the remains of some wild flowers that have been churned to mush under the tyres of at least nine school coaches. He says nothing, because nobody would care, but his blood seems to speed up, gushing through his body like water through a garden hosepipe. Unable to look at the destruction any longer, Josh glances back into the bus and does a double take, when he notices that Mr Brown looks tense.

"Old Beigey knows," he thinks, when his eyes connect, fleetingly, with the teacher's. "He knows that this is all wrong."

At the far side of the farmyard, some cows have gathered in the corner of a waterlogged field. They are agitated and bellowing to their calves, who are in a different field, with their ears tagged, ready to be taken to the market. Fidgeting and huffing, Josh presses his hands tight against his ears, but the animal's cries are too loud, and he cannot shut them out.

By now his blood is sizzling so much that he can feel it firing through his entire body, like electricity. He begins to tremble as the pressure inside him builds until he can contain it no longer and his temper erupts like the spout of a boiling hot fountain.

"Torturers!" he yells, at the top of his voice, not meaning to actually say it out loud, because he really isn't all that brave.

Glancing up from his clipboard, the fed-up looking bus driver gives him a funny look. But people often do that to Josh, and he is used to it, so he fiddles with his glasses, pretending to clean them, pretending not to notice the bus driver's bemused expression.

When, at last, twenty-nine excited school children are organised into a line, ready to be marched off the long school bus like a parade, Josh holds back. Waiting at the end of the queue, he watches the girl at the front. She is smiling as she skips down the steps before jumping into the mud and deliberately, with her feet together, causing an enormous splash.

"Oh grow up," mutters Josh, tutting and searching his brain to find a plausible excuse not to follow them. He is considering faking a stomach ache when, from nowhere, an oddly thrilling thought pops into his head.

"You know that if you wanted to," his own voice is telling him, "if you really wanted to, you could just be brave and do what you believe to be the right thing. It's not that difficult."

In an instant Josh makes the nerve-racking decision to confront the teacher. Never, in his entire life, has Josh ever disobeyed an order from a person in authority. Ever! He has far too much respect for rules to even think of it. But today is different. Today Joshua Beadle is going to say NO. Hardly able to hear a sound above the noise of his own pulse pounding in his ears, he slips back into his seat, digs in his heels and, acting completely out of character, defies Mr Brown.

"Erm, I'm not going in, sir," he says, as calmly as his jangling nerves will let him.

"I'm sorry Josh, but you need to go," says Mr Brown, his thin nasal voice grating on Josh's already over-stretched nerves. "I don't like it either, but we have no choice because the government has insisted."

"Then don't go in," says Josh, struggling to keep his voice steady.

"It's my job, Josh," says Mr Brown, apologetically. "I am sorry, but you really do need to go."

"No!" Josh folds his arms, firmly, across his chest.

Giving in immediately, Mr Brown sighs, his shoulders dropping as he swallows so hard that his Adam's apple moves up and down in his neck. Then, without so much as a nod, he closes his duffle coat toggles, flicks up the hood against the rain, and walks silently off the bus with the rest of the children: steering them through the mud, towards the farm. As soon as the teacher is out of sight, the bus driver turns to Josh.

"Er … erm … be all right on your own for a minute, will you?" he asks, though it is not actually a question, because before Josh can answer he has jumped from the cabin and, with his uniform jacket flapping over his head, is striding towards the farmhouse for an extended coffee break.

Josh sighs.

Left alone in the cold damp bus, he stares out of the window watching stony-faced farm workers, miserable animals and laughing children, all squelching about in the pouring rain. Absentmindedly scanning the area, he notices the long thin body of Farmer McSwiney, draped over the farmyard gate. Surveying his kingdom, the farmer is overseeing the proceedings, watching everything with sharp beady eyes that look as if they have been glued onto his face, either side of a pointed, vulture-like nose. The farmer's wife, who resembles a small orange turnip, is bringing him a mug of tea when she catches sight of Josh, sitting on his own. She nudges her husband.

"Oh no … what now," mutters Josh, his heart sinking, as the two of them squelch through thick sucking mud before Farmer McSwiney stomps into the bus and stands uncomfortably close to Josh's seat.

"You not coming in, son?" says the farmer, cheerfully.

"No!" says Josh, who is not the least bit cheerful.

"Aw, but the little lambykins will be so happy to see you," the farmer's wife shouts from the door.

"Please," says Josh, shaking his head and glaring at her. "Don't patronise me."

Mrs McSwiney looks at her husband.

The farmer shrugs.

"Anyway, boy," he says, dropping his cheerful act, "you've got to come in. The government says so. You had better come along. NOW."

"No!" says Josh.

"You'll get into trouble," says the farmer.

"No!"

Farmer McSwiney leans so close to Josh's face that he can hardly breathe, and he draws back until his skull is pushing hard against the window.

"Get off this bus you little rat," the farmer hisses into Josh's right ear, "If you don't, I will personally see to it that you get into deep trouble with your school. Get it?"

"You, sir, are a bully," says Josh, nervously uncrossing his arms, in case he needs to defend himself, and keeping his voice as steady as he can. "And y…you don't f…frighten me."

"Now, listen to me you little …" snarls the farmer, grabbing the end of Josh's school tie and pulling it towards himself, until Josh feels almost throttled.

Terrified of what the farmer might do next, Josh immediately points to a CCTV camera that is scanning the full length of the bus. The farmer stops dead, his half closed little eyes darting from Josh to the camera and back again before a thin icy smile spreads across his face.

"Come along, young man, you'll enjoy yourself," he says, loudly, keeping one eye on the camera as he carefully smooths Josh's tie against his school shirt.

Saying nothing, Josh stays put and re-crosses his arms, in a gesture of his new found defiance. He tries hard to look menacing, but his face can only manage a half-hearted smirk, which infuriates the farmer even more. Farmer McSwiney's jaw tightens and he hesitates for a moment, sheer hatred glowing from his eyes, his mouth twitching with suppressed rage. Muttering and gesticulating, he stomps back off the bus, shoving his wife out of his way before wading through the mud, towards his farm.

Grateful to be left alone, Josh sighs with relief and wonders if he might have what it takes to become some kind of an activist. But the voice that had encouraged him earlier has gone, and, deep down, Josh knows that he just isn't brave enough for that. Feeling utterly useless, he is drifting into his favourite parliamentary daydream, when the door flies open and Polly and Angela are pushed onto the bus.

"Right! You two can wait in here," says a furious, grey-haired teacher, her tweed skirt and wax jacket caked with mud. "I will deal with the pair of you later."

Polly is rubbing her eyes.

Angela's hands are clenched into tight, painful fists and her face is set in a stony frown.

The girls' muddy boots squelch along the aisle, as they make their way to the seat opposite Josh. Trembling with a mixture of anxiety and cold, they take off their dripping wet jackets and set about comparing goose bumped forearms. They look up when Josh coughs. Glancing over at him, the girls nod briefly, and then sit side by side, shivering on the cold, plastic-covered seats.

Angela speaks first.

"Don't cry, Polly," she says. "Crying won't help. We need to do something, Pol. We need to think!"

"Hello," says Josh. "Are you conscientious objectors?"

For a moment the girls look at each other, trying to work out what a conscientious objector could be.

"Yes," they say, uncertainly, in unison.

"I think so," adds Polly.

"We were upset by what we saw in there," says Angela, "and then a farm worker came over and pulled a tiny lamb by the ear. It was horrible."

"I'm afraid I lost my temper and kicked him," says Polly, biting her bottom lip, her mouth curving into a hint of a smile.

"Kicked him!" says Angela. "She only went and pushed him into the trough. He was soaked. She stood up to him. She was brilliant."

"He only fell over because he was drunk," says Polly, sniggering.

"Wasn't he furious though?" says Angela, bursting into a fit of laughter so hearty that Polly can't help joining in, and Josh finds himself laughing with them.

"I have two gorgeous pigs, you see," says Polly. "I wish people would stop eating animals … you know?"

"The only way to change anything is through politics," says Josh, emphatically.

Frowning, Polly and Angela shoot a sideways glance at each other. Neither of them knows a single thing about politics, and they can't work out how to respond to Josh's remark. The conversation stops with embarrassing abruptness, and, unsure of themselves, the girls stare at Josh, who fiddles with his glasses, pretending to clean them with the end of his school tie.

The awkward silence is broken when the back doors of the bus are flung open with a dull thud, followed by the clatter of the tail-lift being lowered. At the same time the front door folds open, and in walks Peter, who nods at Josh, Polly and Angela, as he makes his way along the aisle, to the back of the bus. Raising her eyebrows, Angela digs an elbow into Polly's rib cage. Instantly, Polly's cheeks turn bright scarlet and she spins around, turning to face the front of the bus, blushing from ear to ear.

"DON'T SHOVE!" Noah's bossy voice roars from the back. "My wheels are stuck in this awful flaming mud. WAIT! You're ruining my chair, for pete's sake. I said WAIT!"

The tail-lift mechanism whines and creaks, raising the platform up to the level of the door so that Noah can roll his expensive sports wheelchair, now covered in thick mud, onto the bus.

"You okay, Noah?" asks Peter.

"I'm fine, no thanks to this lot!" says Noah. "Fancy forcing us to come to this flaming place. Look at the state of my gloves. I thought schools were supposed to educate kids, not flipping well brainwash them."

"Shhh, Noah …" says Peter, smiling weakly and glancing over his shoulder at the others, embarrassed by Noah's outburst.

But Josh's ears prick up because he recognises what he hopes is a kindred spirit.

"Flaming farms!" Noah continues to complain, whilst manoeuvring himself into the wheelchair space at the back of the bus, trying to avoid an elbow injury.

"It's a nightmare," says Peter, quietly taking the seat beside him.

"I hate animal farms," says Angela, who is on her feet and facing the boys at the back of the bus. "I do, don't I, Pol?"

"Me too," says Polly, nodding but facing the front, to hide her blushing cheeks from the boy of her dreams.

Standing up, Josh turns and kneels on his seat, leaning on the head rest, to face Noah and Peter.

"We're conscientious objectors," he says. "We didn't go in because we don't agree with farms, so we objected … we …"

"Yes, all right, all right, I know what a conscientious objector is," snipes Noah.

"Noah!" snaps Peter, glaring at him.

"Oh, I'm sorry," says Josh. "I … I just thought I ought to explain."

"No, I'm sorry," says Noah, sighing deeply. "I shouldn't have snapped. It's been a really difficult day. I'm Noah and this is my mate, Pete."

Peter nods hello, and the five new friends introduce themselves.

Angela looks at Noah.

"I know you from the skateboard park," she says. "Didn't you save that tree?"

"Yeah," says Noah, "with a lot of help from Pete. You've got that wildlife hospital in your garden shed, haven't you?"

Angela nods.

Steeling herself, Polly summons the courage to turn around and look directly at Peter.

"I've seen you, at the skate park … with your shopping trolley," she says, hoping for an explanation.

Peter nods but says nothing.

"Oh, for pete's sake put them out of their misery, Pete," says Noah. "He collects food donations in it, and then gives it away to some homeless people in town. He's bloomin' obsessed with it."

Embarrassed by the attention, Peter lowers his eyes and smiles, shyly. Polly can feel her heart doing flips, and she thinks that she might be falling in love.

"I'd like to stop people eating animals," says Josh, "because it really is barbaric."

"Well, here's the person to speak to," says Angela, nudging Polly. "She got our school to do veggie lunches. Didn't you Pol?"

"We did it together, and we had a lot of help," says Polly, enthusiastically. "It was for my pigs really … and the other field animals."

"At least you have all done something," says Josh, feeling even more of a failure. "All I do is talk, you see … and that's no help, is it … not really?"

"Talking is good, Josh," says Angela.

"Field animals need someone to speak up for them," says Polly.

"So do hungry people," says Peter.

"So do the trees and the environment," says Noah. "And wildlife, come to that."

"I suppose so," says Josh. "But I really think …"

Before he can finish his sentence, the door at the front of the bus is flung open and everyone looks round to see a girl, crouching low to the floor, next to the driver's cabin. Wet, mud-splattered hair hangs over her enormous, steel blue eyes, almost obscuring them, and she is panting for breath, her legs folded under her body, giving the impression of a hunted animal preparing to spring.

"Erm … are you a conscientious objector?" asks Josh. "That means that we …"

"I know what it means," says the girl, kindly. "And, yes, I suppose I am, except …"

Peter freezes and Polly is disappointed to see his face light up, his lips forming a strange lopsided smile as his eyes linger, studying every inch of the girl's face. He is obviously spellbound.

"I'm Peter," he says, trying to swallow, though his mouth is much too dry for that. "And this is Noah, Josh, Polly and Angela."

"*Oh, I know who you are, all right,*" thinks Jet, scanning each of their faces and remembering them from her meditation vision. "*Well, well, well … so this is how we meet.*"

"Err … and you are …?" says Josh, pompously.

"Hmm, oh, sorry, I'm Jet," she says, making an apologetic face. "It's short for Jethro – my horrible parents wanted a boy."

Positioning her head just high enough to let her peer through the bottom of the windscreen, Jet desperately scans every muddy inch of the farm.

"It's not that bad a name," says Peter, wanting to bring Jet's attention back into the bus. "A bit unusual maybe … I mean, your parents can't be that awful … can they?"

"Worse," says Jet, darkly, her head and shoulders suddenly dropping as she pivots on her toes and leaps, arms outstretched, grabbing for the hand rail. "Worse than you could ever imagine … and you're just about to meet them."

The door crashes open and Farmer McSwiney barges onto the bus, leaving his turnip wife standing up to her ankles in thick black mud.

"There you are, Jethro McSwiney," shouts the farmer, ignoring the others and swiping at Jet's clothing. "Get out there and smile at them flaming kiddies."

Grabbing the waistband of her jeans, he hauls her towards the door but Jet clings onto the hand rail.

"I won't do it," she shouts. "You can't make me. I won't do it. GET … OFF … ME!"

Her boot connects with his leg and, clutching at his knee, the farmer overbalances, spins, and falls down the steps, landing face first in the mud. Everyone bursts out laughing. Farmer McSwiney turns purple with rage as his wife cowers, burying her head in her apron. Running up the aisle Jet tries to escape by the bus's back doors, but they are locked from the outside.

"That's … your … parent?" gulps Peter. "The farmer?"

"Afraid so," says Jet, breathless with fear, her body pressed flat against the locked back doors.

In a fraction of a second, Farmer McSwiney is back on the bus. This time he is accompanied by Sam Beggart, a farm worker who fills the whole space with the smell of his underarm sweat. Storming up the aisle, the two men twist Jet's arms up her back and march her off the bus, trapped between them. As she passes Josh, he slips one of his contact cards into the back pocket of her jeans and mouths, "text me." Jet nods over her shoulder before she is hauled off the bus, her father bawling into her face, "YOU'RE GETTING LOCKED IN YOUR ROOM, YOU LITTLE … RAT."

Through the windscreen, the children watch them disappear round the gate, Jet's feet trailing in the mud as she is dragged between the two men, towards the farmhouse.

"Blimey," says Noah, in the silence, after they've gone. "She's the farmer's daughter."

"We haven't seen the last of her," says Josh. "I'm sure of that."

"I hope not," murmurs Peter, wistfully, before turning to Josh. "Why have you got business cards? Do you have a business?"

"These are my contact cards," says Josh, sounding pompous again, and reaching into the inside pocket of his school blazer before offering a card to Peter. "Would you like one?"

"Errrm, sure, thanks," says Peter, noticing that the print on the card is faded, and the edges are torn and dog-eared.

Passing a card to each of the others, Josh asks everyone to keep in touch. And he really means it because, for the first time in his life, he has met people, of his own age, who seem to understand him. He actually wants to be friends with them.

"Anyway, let's forget about this farm and discuss our own project," says Angela. "Is anybody up for that?"

"A project?" says Peter, "To do what?"

"To do something … anything," says Angela. "We could work together."

"But we've all done our bit," says Polly. "What else could we do?"

"I wouldn't know where to start," says Noah.

"We need to talk politics," says Josh, emphatically. "It's the only way. We need to speak to the Government."

"Another campaign," says Angela, ignoring Josh's remark and nudging Polly. "Come on, everyone … wouldn't that be great?"

"I'm with Angela," says Peter. "I vote we do something else,"

"I'm up for that," says Polly, eager to agree with anything that Peter says.

"As long as it doesn't involve the police or the fire brigade or the council … or my mum and dad, come to that," Noah mutters under his breath.

Huddled together in the cold school bus, the five new friends begin to talk, trying to decide on a project that they could tackle as a team. Almost immediately, their conflicting ideas clash so much that Angela's idea of working together seems impossible. Unable to agree on anything, the children sit staring at each other as the conversation dwindles to an uneasy silence. Looking around the group, Josh, the politician, lets out a sigh. He knows that all great plans start with a good idea and, hoping that his parents won't go completely ballistic, he makes another momentous decision.

"Come to my house, everybody," he blurts out, "for a proper meeting … this weekend."

Everybody nods.

"Does this mean that we're real activists now, Josh?" asks Polly, excited by the thought of a new project. Especially one that includes Peter Fairchild.

Josh smiles.

"Yes, Polly," he says, surprise making his voice go up a little. "I suppose it does."

* * * * *

At ten o'clock on Saturday morning, on the top floor of a tall, thin town house, Josh is at his bedroom window, watching Polly and Angela walk up the hill from the bus stop. He loves this particular window because, from it, he can see the rooftop of practically every house in the town.

"One day, when I am the Prime Minister, I'm going to look after all of this," he murmurs, taking in a deep steadying breath and, for the first time ever, rushing down the four sets of stairs to greet his very own invited guests.

His dad meets the girls at the door. Shaking their hands, and then talking nonstop over his shoulder, he leads them along the narrow hallway, towards the dining room at the back of the house.

"I am so pleased to meet you," he says, enthusiastically. "I can't tell you how happy we are that Josh has some friends. Please, please come through."

Peter and Noah receive the same eager welcome, except that the front steps almost stop Noah in his tracks. Josh is embarrassed.

"Oh, Noah," he says. "I completely forgot …"

"No worries," says Noah, preparing to lower himself onto the bottom step. "I can just …"

"Wait, we can lift you," says Mr Beadle, indicating to Peter and Josh, to gather round Noah's wheelchair. "Can't we lads?"

"Lift him?" says Josh, "oh … err … em …"

"Is there a problem, Josh?" asks his dad, adding encouragingly. "Surely us lads can manage that, can't we, boys?"

"Err … sure, Dad," says Josh. "No … problem at all."

But he doesn't mean it, and he stands well back as Mr Beadle and Peter lift Noah up the two steps before they all make their way into the house. Walking backwards and talking all the while, Mr Beadle leads the boys along the cramped little hall, towards the dining room.

"I was just saying to the girls how happy we are to meet you. If I can be of any help, any help at all, you just let me know. Okay? I'll help in any way I can. Just say the word now. Okay?"

"Erm … thank you, Mr Beadle," says Peter, scanning the dining room whilst Josh's dad holds the door open.

"Yeah, cheers," says Noah, casually, over his shoulder, brushing his wheelchair past Mr Beadle's leg.

Peter glares at him.

"What?" says Noah.

The dining room, which is actually a small, inexpensive, extension, has big square windows all around it, making the little room as hot as a greenhouse in summer, and as cold as a fridge in the winter. A glass dining table dominates the space and Josh's mum has completely covered it with a selection of snacks and drinks. Noah sets about transferring himself onto a dining chair and Peter moves the folded wheelchair to a corner, out of the way.

"If you need any more food, just let me know," says Josh's mum. "Don't be shy now. There's plenty more. All right?"

Backing out of the dining room, practically bowing, Mrs Beadle trips over Einstein and topples the coat stand with a loud crash. Josh opens the door.

"Mum, are you …"

"Fine, fine, everything is fine," says Mrs Beadle, getting to her feet as her husband reaches over her, to pull the door closed.

At last, the five young activists are left alone.

"Blimey, Josh, your parents are a bit much," says Noah. "Are they always like that?"

"Yep," says Josh, handing round glasses of orange juice.

"Well, I think they're great," says Peter, adding, "no sign of Jet, then?"

"Nope," says Josh.

"Farmer's daughter," says Polly. "I said she wouldn't come, didn't I, Angela?"

"Stop it, Polly," says Angela. "We don't know anything about her."

"I really thought she would have contacted you," says Peter, his voice quiet. "I was sure that she would …"

"Well, she might text me," says Josh. "You never know … Anyway, if everybody is ready, let's get to work."

Angela speaks first.

"Well, I think we need to stop building houses everywhere," she says, "… and roads."

"People need somewhere to live, Angela," says Peter. "We need houses … and transport, come to that."

"But we need to remember that we share this planet," says Noah, "if we carry on harming the environment then we'll all suffer … in the end."

"I know that, Noah," says Peter. "But we should share resources with other people as well. It's not just about animals and trees. I mean …"

"People need to stop ripping up the natural environment," yells Angela, cutting Peter off. "We're supposed to protect it."

"Angela," snaps Peter. "You can't blame people because they need homes and food."

"Animals are NOT food!" shouts Polly, suddenly on her feet and leaning across the table, her finger prodding at Peter's chest. "If your precious people would stop eating animals then your precious environment would be a lot better off."

Angela opens her mouth to speak.

Polly talks over her.

"Shut up, Angela, it's my turn," she says. "I hate this division between so-called farm animals and wildlife. Or pets that are pampered and cared for. No one gives a hoot about farm animals … or chickens."

"Polly, I'm on your side with that," says Peter, patiently. "I'm just saying …"

But Polly hasn't finished.

"… all this talk about sharing! Well, what's their share … hmmm? All I can see is the abattoir for them. How is that sharing, hmmm … tell me that, why don't you … Peter!"

Eyes wide and blazing with rage, Polly glances around the table, suddenly realising that everyone is staring at her. Shocked by her outburst, she swallows and slumps into the chair, managing to fight back her tears but unable to stop the corners of her mouth from turning down; her bottom lip trembling.

"There's no point in talking to you, Polly," says Peter, quietly.

"Ooooh! Go Polly," says Angela, sniggering. "Listen to you!"

A wave of embarrassed laughter washes over the group, but it fizzles out as quickly as it starts. Left questioning their new found friendships, the children self-consciously avoid each other's gaze until Josh, who has been busy taking notes, finally looks up from his laptop.

"Wow, that was fantastic guys," he says, adding, " what a brilliant debate."

Everybody turns to look at him.

"Fantastic?" says Noah. "All we did was argue. It was a disaster."

"Well, yes," says Josh. "I'll give you that. We'll need a bit more give and take if we are to reach an agreement, but I think we all know that by now."

Peter nods.

"You're right, Josh," he says, casting a meaningful glance in Polly's direction.

"Look, I'd like to try distilling everyone's views into a single plan," says Josh, grateful for the chance to use his political knowledge. "A sort of manifesto for the group. It might help us to see our way forward a bit more clearly. Does that sound okay?"

A vague murmur of agreement drifts around the table.

"Good," says Josh. "Now, let's get some more of my mum's lovely food, and then we can decide when to meet up again."

They are helping themselves to a huge bowl of pakora and more drinks when, without any warning, Mr Beadle bursts into the dining room, assuring everyone that he "absolutely was not" listening at the keyhole.

"Well? How did it go?" he asks, a little too eagerly.

"We argued," says Noah, "... a lot!"

"I certainly hope so," says Mr Beadle. "It's a complicated subject. People have been trying to sort it out for years and my own generation has failed ... really quite spectacularly. But young people, like you guys – well, you're our last hope."

"But there's such a lot to think about," says Polly.

"You'll get there," says Mr Beadle. "If you just work together and don't give up."

"Thanks, Mr Beadle," says Peter. "We'll try to work it out."

"Sorry, everyone," says Polly, red faced, "... for losing my temper."

"Humph," says Noah, turning his head to look out of the window.

Peter glares at him.

"Come on, Noah," he says. "This is important."

Tutting, Noah looks across at Polly and half-heartedly tilts his head upwards.

When, at last, the children have run out of things to discuss, the meeting draws to an uneasy close. Without saying another word, the friends get up and shuffle around the table, squeezing past each other in the tight little space, finding and putting on their jackets. Settling himself back into his wheelchair, Noah pulls on his gloves, ready for the journey home.

Everyone is acutely aware that nobody is speaking.

They don't quite understand it, but they know that something very special – something important – has just happened.

They can feel it.

They are not the same ordinary children who met in the dining room that morning. The whole universe has shifted. Changed.

And it cannot go back.

Raising their hands in a goodbye wave, the friends turn and, without saying a word, make their way down the neat gravel driveway, towards the street. Energy is crackling through their bodies with a force so strong that it feels like electricity firing in their veins, making them powerful and somehow … connected.

Unable to stop grinning and feeling extremely proud of himself, Josh watches his new friends walking down his drive.

For the very first time in his life, he has not been excluded. He actually has an important role in this group. Feeling exhilarated and alive, Josh crosses his fingers before calling after the others:

"Same time next week?"

Chapter 5

WARRIORS

The voice comes out of thin air. It is not in Jet's head, and she is not meditating, so she knows that she couldn't have imagined it.

"Same time next week … for what?" she murmurs, barely moving her lips, her mind grasping at thoughts that are too hazy to reach, like a half-remembered dream. Slumping onto her bed, she picks up her favourite amethyst crystal, absentmindedly allowing her fingers to curl around the coolness of the stone.

"Something … I should know something … but what?"

In a heart-stopping flash, Polly, Peter, Angela and Noah crash through her mind's eye. No blurry television screen this time. This time they are real and, this time, Jet knows exactly who they are. It is when they turn back, raising their hands to wave at someone, that a jolt shoots through her body, arching her spine with such force that her fingers spread in a momentary spasm. Slipping from her grasp, the smooth lilac crystal hits the wooden attic floor with a loud echoing bang before skidding out of sight.

"BE QUIET UP THERE!" her father's voice booms from the ground floor.

"SORRY," Jet shouts distractedly, dropping to her knees and searching about under the bed, for the stone that seems to have disappeared. She sits back on her heels.

"*Hang on a minute … where was Josh?*" she thinks, "*Why don't I see him?*"

Slipping a hand under her pillow, she feels for his crumpled contact card and holds it to the light, her thumb moving over the creases. Jet desperately wants to text him, but she is locked in her bedroom, and this time her parents have taken her phone. Ordinarily she would have escaped along the edge of the roof and down the drainpipe, but the guttering has been removed for repairs, and, for the moment, she is stranded.

Looking towards the corner, she considers the flickering silver sparkles that twinkle and dance about her guardian angel.

"Why have you brought these ordinary kids into my life?" she asks. "I don't get it. I wish you would help me to understand."

As usual, the angel-light says nothing, but Jet is convinced that these four children must be important … must be Indigo. She can feel it. She can feel … them. Clasping her hands, she raises them to her chin and makes a silent vow to meet these children again … no matter what it takes.

Sliding an ancient laptop from its hiding place under the bed, she hits the 'on' button. The screen glows and Jet sets it aside whilst the equipment starts up, beeping and whirring into life.

She studies Josh's cheerless little contact card. No email, no address, only a mobile phone number for the boy who calls himself 'Master Joshua Beadle.' The old fashioned formality of the words makes Jet smile, but only for a moment, because she needs to get her hands on a mobile phone. She doesn't have time to waste.

Balancing the old computer on her knees she hunches over it, fingers deftly skipping across the little grey keyboard, composing a quick email, asking for help. A click on the 'send' button and the message is flying through cyberspace, taking Jet's plan to her trusted friend Chrissie, who never lets her down.

* * * * *

At one-thirty in the morning, the moon hangs bright and clear against the black night sky. Standing at her attic window, Jet surveys the empty fields until she spots three figures, coming together on the road at the bottom of the lane. They are riding a bicycle and a tandem.

The bike belongs to Chrissie.

The tandem is ridden by the Quinn twins, Todd and Owen, who do not look remotely like brothers, let alone twins. But the boys are close ... so close that they sometimes speak almost in unison, except that Owen lags behind, like an echo.

"Thanks guys, I owe you one," murmurs Jet, though she knows that her friends cannot hear her.

She glances over her shoulder at the dark little corner. No sign of the guardian angel. All that Jet can do is watch and pray that her allies will not be discovered.

As they approach the farm lane, Todd switches off the cycle lamp and the tandem travels the last few metres bathed in silver moonlight.

He has no trouble identifying the run down old farmhouse because its outline is clearly visible from the road. On one end of the roof, a weather vane witch sits on a long broomstick, her pointed hat and arched hissing cat cast in shadow against a huge floodlight of a moon.

Todd shudders.

When she sees the tandem, Chrissie rolls her eyes.

"What is that contraption?" she asks, flatly.

"It's a tandem ... tandem," say the twins, not-quite-in-unison.

"Haven't you seen a tandem before?" asks Todd.

"Of course I've seen one before," says Chrissie, through gritted teeth. "I meant what's it doing here! We're going into Jet's dad's farm in the middle of the night. You know how dangerous that could be and you've brought a tandem! What were you thinking?"

"Isn't it fantastic though?" says Owen, proudly. "We found it in a scrap yard, and fixed it up, didn't we Todd?"

His brother nods, enthusiastically.

Chrissie rolls her eyes again.

"If you say so," she sighs, knowing that there is no point in arguing with them. "Come on."

Hiding the bikes by a loose wooden gate, Chrissie, Todd, and Owen, clamber over it and start up the lane, single file, towards the house. The lane quickly dwindles to a stony, rutted, dirt track. Staying close to the hedges and moving as fast as they can on the rough uneven ground, the three friends creep along the track until, at last, they reach the farmhouse.

Rusty, the farm collie, is dozing in her kennel when she catches Chrissie's familiar scent. Lifting her head to sniff the night air, the elderly dog scrambles to her feet and hobbles silently towards the intruders, wagging her tail between stiff, arthritic legs.

Cringing at every little noise, Chrissie and Todd slip past the side gate, make their way round to the back, and wait, straining to listen for any sign of movement coming from the house. Tiptoeing around the corner behind them, Owen glances up and spots Jet standing at her window. Smiling up at her, he raises his hand to give a thumbs-up before walking straight into an old oil drum, knocking it over with an almighty clatter. The sound of metal on stone vibrates through the night-time silence with exaggerated loudness as the empty container rolls the full length of the yard, rattling over the uneven paving before crashing to a halt against the wooden picnic table.

Instantly, the friends press their bodies flat against the rough, grey sandstone wall and stand perfectly still, hidden in the shadow of the building. Terrified, they grasp at each other's hands, clasping them as they wait in the darkness, joined together in a futile gesture of solidarity. As fast as her painful joints will carry her, Rusty shoots back to the safety of her kennel as a light goes on in the downstairs bedroom.

Gasping, Jet slaps a hand to her mouth and closes her eyes, trying to listen over the deafening sound of her own heartbeat. A barely audible whine escapes from her lips when she hears heavy footsteps stomping about on the ground floor.

"Oh, no," she murmurs, glancing at the dark corner, challenging the seemingly absent guardian angel. "Do something! For heaven's sake, help them!"

"WHERE DID I PUT THAT GUN?" Farmer McSwiney is complaining loudly.

Then Jet has an idea.

Almost numb with fear, she knows that, if her angry father takes one step outside of the house, he will shoot randomly into the darkness before any questions are asked. With trembling hands she throws her canvas tote bag out of the window and lowers it down to the ground, on a long string. Then, taking a quick determined breath, she scoots over to the bedroom door, screws her eyes shut and kicks it, as hard as she can.

Instantly, her father's footsteps stop and his wild animal roar, like the terrifying growl of an angry bear, fills the entire house. Squeezing herself into a corner of the room, Jet tries desperately to work out her father's movements as she waits for the onslaught. Then her heart sinks when she hears a familiar sound. Thud after thud, heavy footsteps pound the wooden stairs towards the attic. It is a sound that Jet has come to dread.

Curling her body into a tight ball, she wraps her arms around her knees and listens to the key turning in the lock before the door is flung wide open. The light from the stairwell casts a gigantic shadow that seems to fill the whole room with her father's overbearing presence. His face distorted with rage, the farmer swipes Jet from the floor and hurls her across the room, as if she was a rag doll. Airborne, she is flying straight for the corner when the angel-light flashes for a second, blocking her path. Suddenly veering to the right, Jet bounces onto the bed, her shoulder smacking against the wooden pallet headboard, a sharp pain jarring her neck. In two strides her father has crossed the bedroom. He grabs at Jet's hair, tangling it through his fingers, pulling her towards him, as she cowers in her duvet.

"What do you think you're doing, you selfish little rat?" he snarls.

"I'm … I'm … feeling sick," says Jet. "Yes … that's it … I thought I needed help. I thought I was going to … to pass out."

"Well pass out, why don't you," bawls the farmer. "Then we might get some sleep around here."

"Yes, I'm really sorry. I didn't mean to wake you. I thought Mum would …"

"You thought nothing! You never think. You're too stupid to think," he prods her bruised shoulder so hard that she reels backwards, almost falling from the bed.

"Yes!" she says. "Yes, you're right. I'm just a stupid girl. I'm sorry."

The farmer's throat vibrates a low primitive growl as he releases his grasp. Snatching up Jet's precious dragon hand mirror, he hurls it to the floor, shattering it, before stomping out of the room and taking care to lock the door behind him.

Swallowing, to avoid throwing up, Jet sits perfectly still and listens to her father making his way down the stairs. For a few moments there are raised voices in the ground floor bedroom, but they muffle when the door is slammed and stop with the click of the light switch.

Grateful for the silence, Jet draws in a long trembling breath. She knows that she has gotten off lightly this time, and she has managed to create a distraction to save her friends.

"Thank you," she says to her guardian angel, though it is nowhere to be seen.

Going to the window, Jet pulls on the string, to retrieve the tote bag as she watches her friends haring down the lane to where they have hidden the bikes. As quickly as they can, they vault over the gate, crank the pedals and speed away, into the night.

Fumbling in the little bag, Jet pulls out some money and a phone with a post-it note stuck to it that reads: "Stay safe Jet xxx." In the darkness of her little attic bedroom, clutching the phone to her chest, Jet smiles.

"At last," she murmurs, "I can text Master Joshua Beadle."

✳ ✳ ✳ ✳ ✳

By Friday morning, the clouds have broken and sunshine floods the little yard at the back of the farmhouse. Farmer McSwiney has taken some lambs to the market and everyone is relaxed when Sam and Nat Beggart arrive to repair the gutter. Alone and forgotten, Jet watches from her little window high on the roof, as the brothers spend a couple of hours unpacking tools and discussing how to tackle the job. Mrs McSwiney brings endless cups of tea and plates of biscuits until Nat checks his watch.

"Time for lunch," he says, as they lay down their tools and head towards the barn. "Time for sandwiches ... and a snooze."

After lunch, the brothers flick on the radio, choose their favourite music station, open some cans of beer and get to work. The gutter is quickly forgotten.

"Care to dance, my beauty?" Sam asks Mrs McSwiney, taking off an imaginary hat and sweeping his arm wide, his body doubled up in a low, theatrical bow.

"Oh, you are a one, Sam Beggart," says Mrs McSwiney, beaming as she offers her small plump hand, and Sam wraps his arm around her waist, as far as it can fit, to lead her in the dance.

Standing on the picnic table, holding an upturned shovel to his chin, Nat pretends to play the fiddle, stomping his foot in time to the music as the square dance caller sings from the radio, "Swing your partner round and round, mosey up and mosey down ..."

Caught up in the moment, Sam and Mrs McSwiney are jigging and dancing all over the yard, her plain practical skirt flying about her knees, when Nat loses his footing and falls off the table, landing on top of the dancers. Fuelled by alcohol, they all run backwards, spilling beer everywhere, and ending up in the ornamental pond, soaked and helpless with laughter.

Taking a hand each, Sam and Nat try to pull Mrs McSwiney out of the pond but she falls back in with an almighty splash! The three of them are laughing wildly, when ... CRASH!

The radio is flung against the wall and bits of plastic fly into the air, scattering jagged black shards all over the yard. Farmer McSwiney is standing in the kitchen doorway.

"What the devil is going on here?" he shouts.

"We were just messing about, love," says Mrs McSwiney, smoothing her wet skirt. "It won't happen again."

"No harm done, eh?" says Sam, gathering up his tools. "Gutter's almost ready. Isn't it Nat?"

His brother nods.

"Humph," says the farmer before addressing each of them in turn.

"You … kitchen," to his wife.

"You … work," to Sam.

"You … help him," to Nat.

Keeping their heads down, the three of them scurry about their work, but not before Sam gives Mrs McSwiney a secret wink and she smiles back, as she scuttles into the house behind her husband.

Unseen in her dark little bedroom, Jet listens anxiously as the brothers finish the gutter, say their goodbyes and then stagger, arms around each other, towards their van. Now all she has to do is choose her moment of escape.

* * * * *

The alarm beeps at half past four on Saturday morning and Jet's hand shoots out, immediately hitting the stop button. Lying fully dressed under the duvet, she holds her breath and listens. The silence tells her that her parents are still asleep. Sighing, she throws the duvet aside and then slides out of bed, her bodyweight making the floorboards creak as she pulls on her trainers. Glancing at the dark, empty corner she frowns.

"Typical," she murmurs.

Opening the window, Jet ties her rucksack onto some string and drops it over the side. Feeding the string through her fingers, she lowers the bag until it reaches the ground, before taking hold of the window frame and stepping onto the ledge. Crouching there for a moment, she checks along the length of the roof, inspecting the guttering. Sam Beggart can never be trusted to do a good job, and Jet can't be sure that the new gutter will be strong enough to hold her weight. Putting one foot onto the plastic pipe, she gives it a push. It holds. She pushes harder. It still holds.

"It's okay," she tells herself, as she moves her trembling body away from the safety of the window ledge. "It'll be fine … I think."

Balanced on the gutter, Jet glances at the stone slabs in the yard, far below. Almost immediately, she feels the thin plastic pipe bending a little, moving under her feet, as if it is going to give way. Terrified, she sits back onto the window ledge, gasping a few short breaths. But there is no choice because this is her only way out of the house. She has to try again.

Praying that she will not crash to the ground, Jet steps back onto the gutter and, thankful that it hasn't rained overnight, she slips her foot into the open trough. It groans a little but, to her great relief, it holds her weight. Placing one foot directly in front of the other, arms outstretched, Jet inches along the gutter, balancing like a tightrope walker. Her confidence returns as she glides, seemingly effortlessly, towards the forgotten old satellite dish that is still attached to the corner of the building. It is almost within her reach.

"Just a few more steps," she murmurs, "and I'm safe."

Sighing with relief, she extends a hand towards the dish when, to her horror, the groaning plastic gutter gives way and she can feel it buckling and crumpling under her feet. In a panic, Jet throws herself forward and she is in mid-air when the gutter completely dislodges, swings away from the wall and, taking a few roof tiles with it, ends up sticking straight out like a flag pole.

Stretching as far as she can, she grabs for the dish, her fingertips just making contact with the bracket. Her arms take her full weight, every muscle juddering with pain, as Jet hooks her fingers over the rail, and her body thuds against the wall. Scrabbling frantically, her feet scratch against the drainpipe until her toes find the edge of a support clip and she balances on it, like a rock climber. The relief is instant as the muscles in her arms start to relax.

Twisting her neck to look over her shoulder, Jet watches as the new gutter support falls to bits, leaving the cheap plastic pipe dangling down the back wall. Clinging to the rail, she holds her breath and listens for the familiar thud of her father's heavy footsteps. To her relief, the only sound that she can hear is the usual early morning birdsong. She breathes out.

Then, in the half-light of the morning, Jet slithers down the drainpipe, steps onto the water butt and jumps to the ground, as silent as a cat.

Glancing up at the cheap plastic gutter that is dangling from the roof, Jet feels a tingle of fear crawl up her spine.

"*So much for Sam Beggart's handiwork,*" she thinks. "*I'll probably get the blame for that. Oh well, I'll just have to face Dad's wrath when I get home.*"

In her mind's eye she can picture him already. Fists flying in the air, red faced and roaring like a mad man. She wonders how anyone can live like that. Jet sighs.

"*Hey ho,*" she thinks, "*this meeting had better be worth it.*"

Picking up her rucksack, she secures the straps over her shoulders before trotting along the farm track and down the potholed lane, to start the long walk into town. Her mood is unusually cheerful. She has a good feeling about the people she is going to meet today, because she is sure that their coming together, on that school bus, was no fluke. How could it be?

When, at last, she strolls into the quiet, early morning, bus station, Jet's empty stomach starts to complain. Slipping off her rucksack, she says a quiet thank you to Chrissie, unzips the pocket where she keeps her money and counts some change. Her thoughts begin to race. Could these kids have a special purpose? Jet really believes that they do, though she has no idea what it could be. Heading straight for the station snack bar, to buy some breakfast, Jet hopes that she is about to find out.

* * * * *

In preparation for Josh's meeting, Mrs Beadle has arranged snacks and drinks on the glass dining table, and her husband has gaffa taped a portable ramp over the front door steps. Noah and Peter arrive first, and Josh is already at the door, eager to escort them to the meeting room.

"What are you grinning about?" Noah asks him. "What's up?"

Before Josh has time to think of a clever answer, they have reached the door to the dining room and so he pushes it open and stands aside.

Peter gasps.

"She's here," he says, in a whisper. "Jet's here."

"Hi," says Jet, smiling warmly at Peter. "You're Noah, right?"

"Nope," says Noah, carefully steering his wheelchair around the edge of the table. "He seems to have lost the power of speech, but he's Pete. I'm Noah."

Jet's self-assured laugh fills the air and Peter's eyes light up as his mouth breaks into a genuine smile so wide that it creases the corner of his eyes. Noah shakes his head, rolls his eyes and tuts, as the doorbell rings and Josh comes in with the girls.

"Great," says Angela, lifting her hand in a friendly wave, "another girl. Hi, Jet."

Resisting a frown, Polly glances at Peter, and then forces a smile at Jet before taking her seat at the table, next to Angela.

Noah turns to Jet.

"How can you bear to live on that farm, with those awful people?" he asks, bluntly.

"Noah!" shouts Peter.

"What?" says Noah.

"It's a fair question, Pete," says Jet. "I've fought against them all of my life, Noah, and they know that I plan to leave as soon as I am old enough."

"Do your parents actually like you?" asks Peter.

"I sometimes wonder about that myself," says Jet, laughing again. "You see, they wanted a boy to work on the farm and they got me. A girl, a vegan and an Indigo. I am your genuine, all round disappointment."

Peter is spellbound.

"Indigo?" he says. "What's an Indigo?"

"Indigos are kids who were born for a purpose," says Jet, getting carried away on a wave of enthusiasm. "Our planet is not being looked after. It needs some help, and Indigos instinctively know it. We can feel it and we want to do something about it. I think that might be the reason why we were brought together on that bus. It wasn't by chance. I think we might have a job to do. I think we are all ... erm ... Indigos."

Noticing that the others are staring at her, Jet stops speaking and, half expecting to be thrown out of the meeting, she waits for a response.

Shaking his head, Josh purses his lips, his eyebrows wrinkling into a deep mocking frown.

"Indigo?" he says, clearly unimpressed. "Really?"

"Indigo, Starseed, Crystal," says Jet, a little less enthusiastically. "It doesn't matter what you call it, because kids all over the world seem to be … erm … waking up and wanting to … well, help the planet … and each other … to do … s … something."

"Save the planet?" asks Noah, struggling to keep up. "How are six kids supposed to do that?"

"You've already started, Noah," says Peter, trying to help Jet. "Saving that tree, remember? You got people to think about it. That's the point, isn't it, Jet? We all need to do something. Anything. No matter how small."

"That's it exactly, Pete," says Jet, grateful for Peter's support.

"Nope, sorry, Jet," says Josh. "You've lost me now. I just don't believe any of that new age mumbo jumbo stuff."

"Yeah, sure, no worries, Josh," says Jet, breezily. "But I think you are Indigo … whether you believe it or not."

"Do you really think that we could make such a big difference?" asks Polly.

Nobody answers Polly's question because, apart from Josh, who is busy re-checking his notes, everyone is trying to take in the thought that they could be an Indigo child … that they might have a duty to help Planet Earth.

It is Noah who breaks the long silence when he comes up with an idea.

"We should have a name for this group," he says, "something snappy like The Activists or The Something Party."

"What about, The World Champions?" says Angela.

"The Veggie Party," says Polly.

"The Parliamentary Party for Action," says Josh.

"Indigos," says Peter, his eyes fixed on Jet. "We should be called Indigos."

"Indigo Warriors!" says Angela, punching the air with her fist.

"What?" says Josh. "Oh, come on …"

"We all like it, Josh," says Noah, smiling, "… and that's democracy!"

"If you say so," says Josh, annoyed that he has been outnumbered.

"Brilliant," says Peter. "It's brilliant."

From across the table, Jet smiles at Peter and his expression softens as he gazes back at her. Lowering her eyes, Polly lets out a deep, heartfelt sigh, and Noah starts to snigger.

Mortified, Peter speaks quickly.

"Well, erm … now that we have a name, what's next?"

"A plan to get our message to the Prime Minister!" says Josh. "I've written the manifesto for the group … for the Indigo-blooming-Warriors. Would everyone like to read it?"

He passes some sheets of paper around the table and then sits perfectly still, anxiously watching the Warriors' faces as they scrutinise his work.

MANIFESTO FOR A BETTER LIFE

We want to live in a world:-

◊ Where people know that kindness makes us stronger and not weaker.

◊ Where everybody respects, and cares for, everybody else.

◊ Where everybody respects our planet and we all look after it.

◊ Where people do not eat, or use, animals, birds, fish or insects.

We want every human and every non-human:-

◊ To live without fear and to be safe.

◊ To have a proper home or shelter.

◊ To always have enough food and clean water.

We really believe that if human beings choose to:-

◊ We can live in peace with each other and all earthling species.

◊ We can stop fighting and having wars.

◊ We can remember to take care of one another.

"Well … ," asks Josh, nervously, "erm … what do you guys think?"

"This is great, Josh," says Angela. "It's a fantastic start."

"It's a bit idealistic," says Peter, doubtfully. "I mean … we could never do that much."

"Of course we won't," says Josh. "It's only a statement of our vision. I know that we need to start small. It's just something that we can take to Westminster … to give to the Prime Minister … that's all."

"This is really good, Josh," says Jet, hesitating, "… but Parliament … I don't know about that."

"The Prime Minister, Josh, are you mad?" says Polly, who is actually really excited by the thought of going to Parliament, "We can't do that … can we?"

"Why not?" says Josh, insistently. "We'll go to Westminster, and take our manifesto into Parliament. Why not?"

"Well, they won't let us in for a start," says Polly. "What about doing something online. A petition campaign … or something."

"I know something that we could do," says Angela, looking at her phone, her finger swiping the screen, "It'd be more like an investigation than a campaign, though. Something I think I might have seen. I'm not really sure. I took a picture but … well, see for yourself."

Turning the screen outwards, Angela holds the phone in her outstretched hand to let the others see her photograph. They look at it and then look, blankly, at one another.

"It's just a picture of a run-down charity shop," says Polly, baffled.

"Is that it?" says Noah. "It's not much, Angela. What are we supposed to do about …?"

"Look in the window," says Angela, cutting him off, "and tell me if you can see a figure in the background?"

"Oh yeah, there is something there … see?" says Jet, straining her eyes and pointing at the screen. "In the corner … at the back … just there."

"Let me see that," says Josh, snatching the phone from

Angela's hand whilst everyone gathers round him to get a better look.

Polly's face twists into a grimace as she takes in a loud, sharp breath.

"Ooooo," she says. "What IS that?"

"I don't know," says Peter. "Some sort of animal?"

"It looks sort of human, to me," says Jet.

"It's too small for that," says Polly, "and look at the way it's hunched up in the corner. It's got to be an animal."

"When have you ever seen an animal like THAT?" asks Noah. "Look at those blood red eyes and those huge teeth."

"And the fingers," says Peter, gulping. "It looks … demonic."

"Alien?" says Jet.

"Ooh, ET!" says Polly, sniggering.

"A goblin," says Angela, waving her fingers in Polly's face. "Or a demon. Wooooo!"

The girls burst out laughing.

"That's not funny, Angela," says Noah, who hates anything to do with ghosts. "It looks evil! I don't think we should even …"

"Oh, for heaven's sake, Noah," says Josh. "Who on earth believes in all that demon rubbish, nowadays?"

"It's got to be a trapped animal," says Angela. "I vote we go and check it out tomorrow."

"Me too," says Polly.

"Tomorrow?" says Jet, hesitating. "I'll try, but, you see, I broke some guttering when I climbed out of the window this morning, so my dad will be mad when I get home. He might lock me in my room for a while … I'll have to see."

"Did you say, 'out of the window' Jet?" gasps Angela. "You actually had to climb out of a window?"

"Does your dad ever calm down, Jet?" asks Josh, remembering his encounter with Farmer McSwiney. "He scared the heck out of me on the bus that day."

"He has a temper, that's for sure," says Jet, her hand rubbing the bruise on her shoulder. "But sometimes my mum can calm him down. I'll speak to her when I get home."

"Well, that's us girls in," says Angela.

"I'm up for it," says Peter.

"Fantastic," says Josh. "A project for the Indigo Warriors."

"What, ghost hunting?" says Noah. "Absolutely no way. No! No way! You can count me out."

"No worries, Noah," says Josh. "Some of us can meet at the shop tomorrow, to check it out. Is everyone happy with that?"

"You lot are flaming nuts," says Noah.

* * * * *

The next day, Josh, Polly and Angela meet outside a grubby little café, directly across the road from the charity shop.

"Do you think Jet will come?" asks Polly.

"She has to come," says Angela, "we're supposed to be the six Indigo Warriors."

"There she is," shouts Josh, his hand flying up, and a finger pointing towards some traffic lights down the road, "I knew she could pull it off."

Trotting over the zebra crossing, Jet hurries up the street to meet the others.

"Sorry I'm late, guys," she says, breathlessly. "Hope you weren't waiting too long."

"You made it," says Polly, adding, "well, tell us what happened … we're dying to find out."

"It was my mum, really," says Jet. "You see, Sam, who did the work, has a crush on my mum. He'd do anything for her. She got him to take the blame for putting up a cheap gutter, AND he's going to fix it for free. So I am off the hook … this time."

"Oh," says Polly, cheerfully, "well your parents can't be all that bad then."

"Well, my mum does her best," says Jet. "She's just scared of my dad's awful temper."

"Right," says Josh, taking the lead. "Let's get some drinks, and check out this charity shop of yours Angela."

In the café, they take the table in a bay window so that

they can study the whole area. From where they are sitting, the charity shop looks derelict. Red paint is peeling away from the door and a plastic banner, announcing 'Animal Assistance Charity,' is flapping loose, over a filthy window of cracked glass panels. Loose bricks in the wall give the impression that the window could fall out at any moment.

"This old place is closed down, Angela," says Josh. "There's nothing happening here."

"You're wrong, Josh," says Angela. "It opens for a couple of hours every Saturday, but it's always empty. I don't know how it makes any money."

"Only one way to find out," says Jet, finishing her drink in one gulp and heading for the door. "Come on."

Following Jet into the street, the Warriors cross the busy road, and gather at the shop front to peer through the dirty window. Old clothes, shoes, and bric-a-brac lie scattered everywhere. A wooden L-shaped counter, with an ancient manual cash register on it, completely fills one corner.

"Let's go around to the back," says Jet, turning towards a narrow, cobbled lane that runs down the side of the building.

"Josh, you're shivering," says Angela. "Are you okay?"

"Of course I'm okay," snaps Josh. "Why shouldn't I be!"

Frowning, Angela looks sideways at Polly, who says nothing, but shakes her head and shrugs. They follow Jet into an alleyway lined with burst and overflowing bin bags, carefully picking their way down the dank little passage. It opens into a dustbin yard, at the back of the shops.

"This must be the back door," says Josh, tugging the handle. "It won't open."

"How do you know that's the right door?" asks Angela.

"Trust me," says Josh, "it is."

"But …"

"It just is. Okay!" says Josh, his voice quivering, fear making him speak louder than he had meant to.

"All right, keep your specs on," yells Angela. "You don't need to shout."

"Shush," says Jet, "you'll …"

"Oi, what's going on here? Who the hell are you lot?" shouts a tall, thin man, in a crumpled shell suit and trainers, who is emerging from the door next to the one that Josh is trying.

Unsure of what to do next, the stunned Warriors hesitate and look at each other, waiting for someone to make a decision.

"Get out of it …" shouts the man, striding towards the children, and waving a cricket bat in the air.

"RUN!" shouts Angela.

Turning on their heels, the Warriors hare back up the lane to the safety of the busy street. They don't stop running until they reach the skateboard arena, in the park.

"Everybody stop!" says Jet. "He's gone. He gave up chasing us ages ago."

Doubled over and gasping for air, Josh frowns at Polly and Angela, who are laughing breathlessly.

"What's so funny?" he says, between breaths, his lungs burning as if they are on fire. "Look, if you're not going to take this seriously …"

"Sorry, Josh," says Polly, her laughter turning to hiccups.

"Hey! Don't you have a go at Polly!" snaps Angela. "I told you that wasn't the flippin' door."

"I made a mistake, okay … I … I'm sorry," says Josh, red faced, his voice breaking.

"Are you all right Josh?" asks Jet. "You're shaking like a leaf."

Polly and Angela stop laughing, and the three girls gather round him.

"Listen guys, I don't think I'm cut out for this activism stuff," says Josh, his mottled red face turning pale and pasty, "I'm a speaker. A thinker, you know? This is too dangerous for me. Sorry guys, but I'm quitting."

"Look, there's Noah," says Jet, changing the subject and raising her hand to wave, calling, "Hey, Noah."

A wide grin spreads across Noah's face as he waves back to Jet. Unclipping his helmet, he lets the chin strap dangle for effect before spinning his chair and cruising through the arena towards the Warriors.

Angela and Polly continue to stare at Josh.

"You can't quit Josh," says Angela, quietly. "We need you. We're the Indigo Warriors, remember?"

"We have a job to do, Josh … it's important," says Polly.

Noah skids to a halt, scattering dirt and gravel over Josh's polished, lace up shoes.

"What's up, guys?" he says, looking around the group, "Jeez, look at your faces. Has something happened?"

"Josh is leaving the Warriors," says Jet, straightforwardly.

"No, he isn't," says Noah, turning his chair to face Josh. "Not allowed, Josh. We're in this together. Even me … and if I can handle a bit of ghost hunting, then so can you."

"Crikey, Noah, Pete was right," says Josh. "You really are bossy."

"Where is Pete?" asks Noah, his eyes still fixed on Josh.

"Doing a car boot sale with his mum," says Jet, "She needed him to carry her stuff."

"Let's go and get him," says Noah, turning his chair. "I think we need to have another meeting."

* * * * *

The car boot sale covers a huge area of the recreation ground next to the sports centre, and it is filled to capacity. The noise, generated by hundreds of haggling voices, deafens the Warriors as they battle through a jumble of folding tables and baby buggies. Thoroughly enjoying the challenge of keeping himself upright, Noah skilfully weaves his wheelchair through the mayhem, happily turning and spinning to avoid collisions.

When Peter notices his friends making their way through the crowds and looking slightly bewildered, he smiles with relief. Waving both hands in the air, he manages to draw their attention, and they immediately change direction, heading straight towards his mum's stall. Peter nudges his mum, who is leaning over an extremely unsteady wooden table that is packed with her home-made jams, marmalade and lemon curd. Mrs Fairchild beams when she sees the Warriors.

"My dearest children," she shouts, "how wonderful to see you all. Have you come to buy my lovely produce? It's organic … and it's all vegan. Don't they look pretty?" She waves a graceful hand over dozens of multi-coloured gingham paper tops that are fastened onto jam jars and secured with elastic bands.

"Hi, Mrs Fairchild," says Noah. "Not at the moment thanks. We've come to see Peter. Can you spare him for a while?"

"Take him, take him," says Peter's mum, smiling at a customer as she hands him some jars. "That will be two pounds fifty, please. Don't be too long Peter, my darling, I need you here."

Removing his money belt, Peter nods, hugs his mum and then leads his friends towards the small portacabin that serves as a makeshift café.

"Don't tell me," says Noah as they make their way to the cafe, "your mum did a jam making class, didn't she … am I right?"

Snorting through his nose, Peter nods as his whole body shudders, trying to stifle a laugh.

The portacabin café is hot and busy, and it smells of bacon butties. Threading their way between the tightly packed furniture, the Warriors pull out white plastic chairs and put their white plastic cups on an unsteady white plastic table. Polly draws her fingers over the grease.

"Oh God, this is disgusting," she says. "It smells of frying pig meat. I feel sick."

"So, what's up?" asks Peter, amid the clatter of sizzling frying pans and boiling tea urns.

"I've decided to join this ghost hunting project," says Noah.

"I've decided to leave the group," says Josh, wrapping his fingers around his plastic cup and lifting it to his mouth.

"No he hasn't!" says Noah, glaring at Josh. "Not really."

"Blimey, I've only missed one morning and everything's changed," says Peter. "What happened?"

"We got chased by a weapon-wielding maniac, is what happened," says Josh.

"It was only a cricket bat, Josh," says Angela, making light of the incident.

Polly is laughing again.

"It was really exciting, Peter," she says. "You should've been there."

Peter and Noah listen as the others recount their story about the charity shop and the man in the purple shell suit.

"Why don't a few of us go back one evening after school," says Peter, "see if we can find out what that shell suit man was up to in there. What do you think Noah?"

Noah nods enthusiastically and, after tipping his cup to get the last drop of tea, says, "yep, count me in."

Josh groans, the blood draining from his face until his lips turn white.

"I think I'll give this one a miss," he says, fiddling with his glasses.

"Oh, come on, Josh," says Noah. "Man up for heaven's sake. It might not even lead to anything. We're only going to have a look, that's all."

"Stop being so bossy, Noah," says Josh, crossly.

Peter smiles.

"Welcome to my world, Josh," he says.

Chapter 6

THE CHARITY SHOP

The following evening Peter, Noah and Jet pick their way around the cluttered little shop, shining torches under heaps of old clothes, books and broken furniture: searching for clues.

"Who on earth would buy any of this trash?" says Jet, holding a stained, torn cardigan by the tips of her fingers. "It's a load of old rubbish."

"Nobody would buy this," says Peter. "But I don't think that's the purpose of this shop."

"It doesn't feel like it's haunted," says Jet, "and that's why we're here, remember. I mean there's no …"

"Shhh," says Noah. "I heard something."

"I didn't hear anything," says Jet.

"Besides," Peter continues, "it's …"

"Shut up, Pete," hisses Noah. "Someone will hear you."

"Oh, right! And who would that be?" says Peter, annoyed. "No one is remotely interested in this old shop. Look how easy it was to open the back door. It was hardly even locked."

"Well, who made that weird scratching noise then?" says Noah, his torch sweeping the pitch black room like a searchlight.

"There was no noise," says Peter. "It was your imagin …"

"There it is again," says Jet, quietly.

"Shhh," says Peter, straining to listen for the slightest hint of movement, "wait …"

Flicking off their torches they wait in the dark, too frightened to move a single muscle.

"Oh, very funny, Pete," says Noah. "Let go of my hair."

"What?" says Peter, shining his torch on his own face. "I'm nowhere near you."

"You then, Jet, cut it out."

"I'm over here," says Jet, moving her face into the torchlight, "… with Pete."

"What! Whoahhh, get off me," cries Noah, flapping his hands hysterically about his head before spinning his wheelchair and heading out of the door as quickly as he can turn the wheels.

"Arrrrgh," shouts Peter, flinging his torch into the air and running after Noah in a blind panic, leaving Jet on her own in the dark, empty, shop.

"Oh, for pete's sake," she mutters, shaking her head before calmly picking up Peter's torch and walking out of the back door, carefully pulling it shut and then trotting up the lane after the boys.

She is two blocks away before she catches up with them.

"What a pair of wusses," she says, striding confidently towards Noah and Peter, who are already arguing. "Some warriors you are!"

"It was him," says Peter, pointing at Noah. "Shooting out of the place like that! You scared the life out of me, you idiot. What got into you?"

"There's something in there, Pete," says Noah, his voice hoarse with fear. "Something grabbed my hair."

"No! It didn't!" says Peter, emphatically. "Because there is nothing in there, you wally."

"Well, we can't be sure about that, Pete," says Jet, handing Peter his torch. "Noah could be right. I'm going back in."

"Well, I'm not," says Noah, securing the brakes on his chair to emphasise the point. "There's something … unnatural in there."

"I'll come with you," says Peter, scowling at Noah before

trotting after Jet and calling over his shoulder. "You wait here … and for heaven's sake calm down."

Peter and Jet make their way back to the shop and tiptoe around in the gloom. Working within the narrow beam of her torch, Jet picks up an old umbrella and hooks the thin crook handle under a filthy sleeping bag. She lifts it up for inspection.

"Peter, look at this," she says, crinkling her nose at the smell, "it's wet and there are fresh droppings stuck to the fabric."

"Something's been sleeping in this," says Peter, meeting her gaze. "Cats? Squirrels, maybe?"

"I don't know," says Jet, peering at the droppings and chewing her bottom lip. "It doesn't look like cat poo. I'll take some samples, and we can check it out."

"Don't touch it, Jet," says Peter, grabbing her outstretched hand. "That stuff could be toxic."

"I grew up on a farm, Pete, I know what I'm doing … honest," says Jet, slipping her hand away with a giggle that almost melts Peter's heart.

"Well, we can take the droppings to Angela and Cher," he says, looking on, as Jet rummages around in the debris before scooping the droppings into an old plastic food container. "They're the wildlife experts. They're bound to know what animal made them."

* * * * *

Peter can hardly wait the few days until the next Warrior's meeting, and he is already speaking as he steps through the door of Josh's dining room, which has become their official campaign headquarters.

"Well, Angela," he asks, "did you guys identify the samples that we got?"

"No, we didn't, sorry," says Angela, shaking her head. "It just looks human. Small, but human. That's all I can tell you."

"Do you think it could be a child?" asks Peter.

"What – a kid living in that place? Are you crazy?" says Josh.

"I don't think that would be allowed," says Polly. "Aren't there services for children?"

"Where have you lot been living?" says Peter, looking around the table, amazed at their simple-mindedness. "There are kids living rough all over the place."

"They could be held there, I suppose," says Noah, thinking out loud "Against their will."

"Slaves," says Angela, running with Noah's idea. "Made to do housework and stuff. I saw that on the news."

"Maybe that's what's in your photo," says Polly, excitedly. "That little human figure in the background?"

"Of course," says Angela, pointing her index finger in the air to emphasise her Eureka moment. "A child slave."

"Let's not get carried away," says Jet, squinting at the girls. "I think we should dig a bit deeper."

"Well, I vote that we tell the police," says Josh, flatly.

"Tell them what, Josh?" says Peter, pointedly. "That we found some poo stuck to a sleeping bag, in a shop that we broke into?"

"Uh, okay," says Josh. "I take your point … but …"

"We need to investigate this by ourselves," says Noah, deliberately cutting off Josh before he can embarrass himself any further.

"Brilliant," says Jet, nodding across at Peter.

"Oh no," says Josh, wearily. "Not again."

* * * * *

Early the next evening, Polly, Josh and Angela gather in the lane, and watch Peter nudging the charity shop door. It doesn't resist, and the hinges grind as the door opens slowly, practically inviting the Warriors to enter. The smell of urine, wafting from inside the shop, almost overpowers them as they slip, unnoticed, into the building.

"Oh, for heaven's sake," says Angela. "What can they be doing in here? It stinks."

"Someone's been here," says Peter, picking up an empty coffee carton. "This wasn't here last time."

"That means something is happening in this place, then," says Polly, proud of her detection skills. "Because they must have had a reason for coming here."

"Yeah, but what?" says Angela, looking around the cluttered room, "Why would anyone be interested in this derelict place? I just don't get it."

"I don't think we should be in here, guys," says Josh. "Isn't this called breaking and entering?"

"We can't be breaking the law, can we?" asks Polly. "I mean, it's obviously empty, right Josh?"

"It's someone else's property, Polly," says Josh, his voice quivering. "If the police knew tha…"

"Shhh," says Angela, "there's someone outside."

Faint, muffled voices are talking in the lane and getting louder as they move in the direction of the shop. Calmly raising his hand, Peter signals to the others to stand perfectly still and wait for whoever it is, to pass by. The voices move closer, until they stop right outside the charity shop door. A man's soft, mumbling tone is being drowned out by the shrill screech of a very angry sounding woman.

"How could you have let this happen, you idiot?" the woman is shouting. "Do you know how much that damn thing is worth? A bloody fortune. That's how much."

"I've said I'm sorry, my little rose petal," says the quiet man. "It wasn't intentional."

"Intentional!" shrieks the woman, as a key is pushed into the lock. "You haven't had a clear intention in your life … do I have to think for everybody … this door feels loose … did you lock it yesterday? Get this lock replaced, we can't risk anyone snooping about in here."

"Yes, my sweetness," says the man, weakly, when the woman stops to take a breath. "Anything to make you happy."

The door hinges creak.

Looking at each other in horror, the Warriors immediately scatter, scrambling to find a hiding place. Scampering into a tiny side room, Peter, Polly and Angela crouch, in a huddle, behind the door.

Panic stricken, Josh feels his chest tighten until he is struggling to breathe. His head swimming and barely able to think straight, he squeezes himself under the shop counter and pulls a tea stained velvet curtain around his body, just as the woman is walking into the room.

"Right, let's get on with this," says the woman, her high heels clicking on the broken tiled floor. "I don't want to stay in this disgusting place a moment longer than I have to."

"I'll check the back room and you check in here," says the man. "She can't have gone far."

Opening the side room door, the man peers into the darkness, squinting through a thin beam of light that is coming from a tiny barred window. Barely two feet to the left of him, crouched in the shadow, the Warriors sit perfectly still, not daring to move a muscle.

"I know you are in here," says the man, creeping slowly into the room, his nylon shell suit rustling. "Come on, sweetie, come to me."

Secreted in the dark corner, the Warriors watch the shell suit man dragging a dog cage into the middle of the room. He turns the cage onto its side, carefully placing some stale bread into the back of it before lifting the wire door and propping it open with a flat piece of wood. Finally he attaches a thin trip wire to the wood and then steps back to admire his efforts.

"There you are my little one," says the man, loudly, turning his face towards the open doorway. "You must be hungry by now. We're going to find you a new mummy and daddy."

"Is it in there?" yells the woman, from the front shop. "Hurry up, you moron."

Half lowering his eyelids, the shell suit man clenches his fists and hisses a curse, under his breath.

"I'm almost done, my love!" he calls through his teeth, before looking around the room and adding, in a whisper. "Please come to me, little one, I'm trying to help you."

After re-checking his makeshift trap, the shell suit man

hesitates for a moment, his chest expanding as he sucks in a long deep breath. Clenching his jaw, he puts one hand into the other and flexes the knuckles with a loud crack. Turning towards the door, his face breaks into a wide smile before he goes back to join the woman in the front shop.

"Well?" demands the woman, as the shell suit man walks towards her. "Did you set the trap for it … with the bread?"

"Of course, my love," says the man, his voice cold and flat, then adding, with genuine concern. "I hope she's okay."

"IT … had better be okay," says the woman, leaning towards the man and jabbing a long pink fingernail into his purple shell suit. "Or I'll have no choice but to report back to You-Know-Who. And we both know what that will mean."

"Erm … who is this Mr You-Know-Who that you keep talking about, my love?" asks the man, his voice quivering.

"You'll know soon enough!" snaps the woman, slipping an enormous white handbag over her bare shoulder, her heels clicking towards the door. "Right, I've had enough of this. I don't care if this one starves to death. Come on."

The door closes and a key is jiggled in the lock. The woman shouts all the way up the lane until her voice fades and, finally, a car screeches away, into the distance. Flicking on their torches, Peter, Polly and Angela look around the little store room.

"Empty cages," says Polly.

"Animals!" says Peter. "They must be keeping animals here."

"Breeders?" says Polly.

"Could be," says Angela. "Puppies … kittens …"

In his hiding place under the counter, Josh starts to whimper.

Exchanging concerned looks the others go into the front shop and pull back the filthy curtain. Josh, still crouched, is hugging his knees to his chest and rocking. Both of his cheeks are soaked with tears; his breath is shallow and erratic.

"They've gone, Josh," says Peter, prising Josh's arms away from his knees and helping him up.

"Josh, we're safe," says Angela.

"I'm okay," says Josh, who is clearly not okay. "It's just … well, why does this have to be us … why can't we let someone else take care of the planet … I'm not really cut out for this …"

"We think it's animals, Josh," says Peter, interrupting him. "Not children."

"Let's go to that café across the road," says Josh, drying his face on his sleeve. "We need to talk."

Abandoning their search, the Warriors retreat from the shop and walk, briskly, across the busy road, to the café. Taking the table by the window, they sip drinks and stare at the seemingly disused charity shop.

"That woman sounded horrible." says Angela, sucking loudly on her straw, draining her glass of cola.

"She's vile," says Polly, frowning at her friend's lack of café etiquette, and adding, "So … what do we do now?"

Before anyone can think of an answer, the shell suit man reappears. This time he is alone and walking quickly down the street. He glances over his shoulder before turning the corner, into the lane.

"I don't get it," says Peter, nonplussed. "I just can't work it out."

"What can they be up to in there?" says Polly.

"If they're hurting animals I'll …" says Angela, slowly, through gritted teeth, her fingernails digging deep into the palms of her hands.

"We need a proper meeting," says Josh, "before this gets out of hand. At my house … Saturday morning? Same time?"

* * * * *

The Saturday meeting is not going well and ice tinkles in Mrs Beadle's glass water jug when Angela's fist thuds onto the table, next to it.

"Calm down, Angela," says Josh, lifting the jug. "You'll break my mum's glass table."

"Is everything all right in there?" Mr Beadle shouts from the hall.

"It's fine, Dad," says Josh, setting the jug on the sideboard. "We're just having another disagreement."

"Good, good. That's the spirit," says Mr Beadle, "let me know if you need any help."

"Sod this Indigo stuff," yells Angela. "If that vile woman is abusing animals, I'm going to stop her ... by force if necessary."

"We really, really need to tell the police, now," says Josh.

"Tell them what?" says Jet, exasperated. "There's no law against breeding dogs and cats for money, and anyway, we're only kids, they won't even listen to us."

"We broke into the place, Josh, we'd be the ones getting into trouble," says Noah, thinking back to his tree climbing campaign, and keen to avoid having any more contact with the police.

"I can't step outside of the law," says Josh. "What's the point of having law makers if we all just do whatever we want? We need people to look up to ... otherwise there's no point in anything."

"Oh, for heaven's sake, Josh," says Jet, losing patience. "Maybe the law makers need to look up to us for a change! Have you ever thought of that? I mean ... our world doesn't only belong to the adults. We live here too, you know! We have a right to ..."

"Actually, you're all wrong!" says Peter, standing up. "What we need to do is gather evidence. If they are doing something illegal in there then we'll need to have proof before we can tell anyone."

"I agree," says Polly, adding, "I'm sorry Angela, but we can't be violent. We're supposed to be the Indigo Warriors."

"Remember our manifesto, Angela," says Josh.

"But, we can't just let them ..." says Angela, almost in tears.

"Look, you're angry, Angela, we understand that," says Noah, "but violence isn't the way."

"Well, you'd all better come up with a pretty great plan," says Angela, flinging back her chair and stalking out, "or I'm going it alone. END OF!"

The letter box rattles as the front door slams shut behind her.

* * * * *

Next day, at the café, Peter sets his shopping trolley
aside and then moves a chair, so that Noah can tuck his
wheelchair in at the table in front of the café window.

"I hate sitting in the street," mutters Noah. "What if it
rains?"

"Stop moaning," says Peter. "You agreed to do this."

"But … a stakeout!" says Noah. "What is this … a 1970s
cop show?"

"Cops and detectives," says Peter, laughing. "Maybe I
should wear a shiny jacket and roll up my sleeves."

"What are you taking about?" asks Noah.

"What?" says Peter. "Surely, you've seen those slick cop
shows. My mum loves that old stuff. It's on our TV all the
time."

"You know that your mum's bonkers, don't you?" says
Noah, his gaze drifting back to the charity shop across the
street.

"I certainly do," says Peter, grinning, "but she's also
brillian…"

"Look!" says Noah. "There's a man in a purple shell suit.
Gawd, is that him? What a creep."

The boys watch as the man hurries along the street,
towards the charity shop, his shell suit jacket distorted by
the large bulge of something bulky hidden inside it. His left
forearm seems to be supporting a weight and his right hand
is clutching the bulge, holding it close to his body. Stopping
briefly, the man looks over his shoulder before breaking into a
jog as he turns down the lane. A few moments later he is back
on the street, checking both ways before scurrying along the
pavement towards the main road, holding an empty plastic
carrier bag, scrunched in his hand.

"Plastic!" says Noah. "Bloomin' plastic! How long does it
take to get the message across about plast…"

"Shut up, Noah," hisses Peter, "and give me the diary.
What time is it? What do you think he had in that plastic
bag?"

"This is nuts," says Noah, taking no notice of Peter.

"Playing cops and robbers won't get us anywhere. I'm beginning to think Angela was right."

"No! She isn't!" says Peter. "Drink up and stop grumbling."

"Wow … did you see that?" says Noah, almost jumping from his chair.

"See what?" says Peter, looking up from his notes, "I didn't see anything."

"In the shop … something moved," says Noah.

"Don't start that again," says Peter. "There's nothing in there."

"Nothing … alive," says Noah, leaning across the table and raising his eyebrows.

"Yeah … bit dramatic there, Noah," says Peter. "We should call another meeting … we need to regroup."

"Agreed, oh great leader," says Noah, putting his hands together and bowing his head.

"I'll text Josh," says Peter, grabbing the shopping trolley and standing up, "to let him know that we're coming."

* * * * *

The boys are first to arrive for the Saturday morning meeting, and when the doorbell rings again, Josh runs to answer it. Flinging the door wide open, he is disappointed.

"Where's Angela?" he asks, standing aside to let Polly and Jet into the house.

Brushing past him, Polly shrugs and makes her way to the dining room.

"Sorry," says Jet, following Polly along the hall, "she's still in a strop about our non-violence policy."

"But she needs to come," says Josh. "How can we be the Indigo Warriors without her?"

"I'll talk to her," says Polly, "but you know how stubborn she is."

Josh and the girls join Noah and Peter in the dining room, and the five Warriors settle down to discuss their findings. This time, there are no snacks or drinks on the table, and they get down to business straight away.

"You said that you saw something moving in the shop, Noah," says Jet. "What do you think it was?"

"I'm not sure," says Noah, "I know this sounds crazy, but it looked like an imp, or a goblin. Like a skinny old man but really tiny."

"Oh, not that again. Imps and goblins! Are you nuts?" says Josh.

"I'm just trying to tell you what I saw, Josh," says Noah.

"No! You didn't!" says Josh. "Now, can we PLEASE have a serious discussion!"

"Why would shell suit man go in with a full plastic bag and come out with an empty one," asks Polly. "Has anybody managed to work that out?"

"Maybe it's stolen goods," says Peter. "Or money."

"Oh yes," says Josh, "… diamonds, maybe?"

"Well, what would that have to do with us?" asks Polly. "We're supposed to be saving the earth not catching jewel thieves."

"I'm not going after any jewel thieves," says Noah. "Do you know what they do to people?"

"How do you know what jewel thieves do to people?" asks Peter.

"I watch television," says Noah, seriously. "Same as you do."

"Oh, don't be so daft," says Polly.

"I'm sorry, Josh," says Jet, "but I think there is, or was, something alive in there."

"Oh, gawd," says Josh. "You want us to go back, don't you?"

"Yep," says Jet, "we need to see what's in there."

Polly grins.

Josh does not.

* * * * *

It is early evening when the Warriors gather at the charity shop's familiar rickety door.

"You'd better give it a really hard push," says Noah, emphatically, "Josh said they were going to fix the lock."

Nodding, Peter puts his shoulder to the door, which does

not resist and flies open. Running head first into the shop he trips over a pink tricycle, is airborne for a split second, and then lands face down on a pile of filthy old clothes. Taken by surprise, the others stand in the doorway, watching him, until Polly runs inside.

"Are you okay?" she asks, helping Peter to his feet.

"For pete's sake, Noah," hisses Peter, picking a dust bunny out of his mouth. "I thought they were going to fix that lock."

"Yeah," says Noah, brushing his wheelchair past him, "so did I."

Peter glares at him.

"Don't blame me," says Noah, pointing at Josh. "He's the one who said it."

"Well, don't blame me," says Josh, looking at Peter. "It was that woman who said it when we were …"

"Will you lot stop arguing," says Jet. "They could turn up at any minute."

"They obviously think they're safe in here," says Polly, "if they leave the lock broken like that."

"Okay!" says Josh, taking charge, "Polly, Jet, you two go and look around that back room. Noah and I will check in here. Pete, you can keep lookout. Is everybody okay with that?"

Accepting their orders, the Warriors disperse, and Peter makes his way to the top of the lane, to keep watch.

"Look at this, Noah," says Josh, lifting a small battered notebook from the counter and holding it up, for Noah to see.

"A blank page," says Noah, rudely. "Yeah, cheers for that Josh."

"Why are you always so sarcastic? It's not funny you know," says Josh. "This page has been torn out, see? But you can still see the indent from the writing that was on it … see?"

"Why are you always so flaming smart?" says Noah, grinning as he takes the book from Josh's hand, "It's an address … a hotel by the look of it."

"Could be a boat," says Josh, earnestly, "or a caravan. People do that you know … name caravans."

"You know, Josh," says Noah, warmly. "If I didn't like you so much, I'd call you a know-all."

"THEY'RE COMING!" yells Peter, bursting into the shop. "They're getting out of a car. They'll be here any minute."

Dropping the notebook, Noah is first to vacate the shop, with Josh running close behind him.

"Polly! Jet! We need to get out of here!" shouts Peter.

Jet puts her head round the door, "But we just need to …"

"NOW!" Peter interrupts her. "NOW!"

Scrambling out of the shop, the Warriors dive into the space behind some enormous black wheelie bins, just before the shell suit man and the vile woman turn into the lane. Her high heels skidding and scratching on the cobbles, the vile woman leans on the man, complaining in her piercing voice, as they make their way towards the charity shop door. Then she disappears into the gloom of the shop, whilst the shell suit man checks the lane in both directions, before silently pulling the door closed, behind them.

As soon as the coast is clear, the Warriors shoot up the lane and cross the road, to the safety of the café.

"I'll get the drinks," says Polly, her whole body shaking with excitement.

"You okay, Josh?" asks Jet, settling into the chair next to him.

"Yes," says Josh, thoughtfully. "I think I am."

"Well," asks Peter, "did you guys find anything?"

"Does an old pack of disposable nappies count?" asks Polly.

"I doubt it," says Noah. "Josh found a note … well, it's the remnants of a note really … an indent I guess you'd call it … but you could still see …"

"Well?" says Peter "Tell us what it said."

"What?" says Noah. "Oh, yeah … it said: Ivory Towers Hotel, Springtown. Sunday. 11.30."

"I know where that is," says Josh. "We should go and check it out."

"Sorry, guys, but I can't go without Angela," says Polly. "She's missing all this excitement."

"That's up to you, Polly," says Noah. "But no violence. She needs to accept that."

"I'll talk to her," says Polly.

✳ ✳ ✳ ✳ ✳

On Sunday morning, smiling sheepishly, Angela follows Polly into the bus station. Springing to her feet, Jet leaves the boys at the table and runs to meet the two girls.

"We've missed you," she says, flinging her arms around Angela. "We really need your feisty energy with us."

"Aw, thanks, Jet," says Angela, returning the hug. "I wanted to come back, but … well … you know."

Squashed around a little coffee bar table, the boys are welcoming Angela back to the Indigo Warriors, when Jet is distracted by a noise like a burglar alarm, ringing inside her head. She wiggles a pinkie in her ear but, to her annoyance, the ringing refuses to subside. Giving up, she turns her attention back to the group, and gasps because they are completely surrounded by a shimmering haze of silver light, like a heat wave rising in the desert.

Unaware of what is happening around them, the Warriors busily pass snacks and drinks across the table, chatting about the prospect of an exciting day ahead of them. Jet, alone, can feel the power from their combined energy fields. She closes her eyes and breathes deeply, savouring this important moment.

"*The Warriors' strength is complete,*" she thinks. "*Whatever this universe wants from us … surely nothing can stop us now.*"

"Listen, you guys," says Angela, breaking the spell. "I am still angry about animals being hurt, but I know that we can't be aggressive. I get it. I said so, didn't I, Pol?"

"To the Indigo Warriors," says Noah, smiling and holding his paper cup in the air, "… back together again!"

"I looked up the hotel on the internet," says Josh, being practical as usual. "It's a really old building and it looks like it's almost falling down. I've bought the bus tickets."

"Oh, well," says Noah, sighing deeply and scanning the station. "I suppose I'd better find somebody to get me on."

"This is just like the first time we met," says Polly, "in the school bus, at that horrible farm, oh, sorry Jet,"

"We've come a long way since then," says Jet. "Who knows, we might even become famous one day."

"Infamous, more like," says Noah, distractedly, craning his neck to look for a station attendant.

The bus crawls in the congested city traffic, eventually passing tidy suburban gardens before leaving the streets behind, and speeding along narrow country roads that seem to slice straight through the smaller towns and villages. When the bus finally stops in Springtown, it is on an extremely busy road, outside a large supermarket. Fidgeting with excitement, the Warriors wait whilst the driver extends his ramp onto a pavement so narrow that the traffic flies past them, only a few feet away.

"There it is," says Josh, pointing to an old, mock Tudor building, painted blue and orange and sitting on a tight corner, at a pelican crossing.

"I thought it would be isolated," says Polly, shouting to be heard above the traffic noise.

"Me too," shouts Angela. "It's so busy. How can they hide anything here?"

"Well, there's a bright light in the corner of the window," says Jet, "so someone must be in the building."

"I don't see any light ... you must be seeing things, Jet," says Josh, over his shoulder, as he heads towards the hotel, adding, sarcastically. "Or maybe it's one of your spooky angel friends come to save the day."

"*Of course!*" thinks Jet, remembering her very first visions of the Warriors, that morning in the attic. "*You're the outsider! You don't believe in anything. That's why my guardian angel couldn't show me your face.*"

"Jet … come on," Angela's voice breaches her thoughts.

"Coming," she says, following the others into the dingy little cave of a café.

They pick a table near the door and, after a heated discussion, order drinks from the waitress, who has grudgingly come out from behind the counter. Rude and uninterested, the waitress's eyes are fixed on her phone as she brings their order. She dumps a tray of drinks onto the table and turns on her heel, leaving the Warriors to pass glasses and crisp bags between themselves. Ignoring them, Jet slowly tilts her head and, half afraid of what she will see, looks up at the high ceiling space where a dozen balls of light are moving and weaving, as if jostling for space. Distant murmurings bear down upon her; faint voices talking over one another, wailing and pleading until, compelled to join them, she lets out a murmur of her own.

"Where are you, guardian angel?" she says under her breath. "I really need you here."

The spell is broken when Josh's voice wrenches Jet away from the gentle spirit voices, forcing her back to the café, back to the Warriors.

"How would a person go about booking a room here?" Josh is asking the waitress, who is slouched over the counter, still looking at her phone.

"Oh … a room is it!" says the waitress, slipping her phone into the pocket of scruffy, ripped jeans. "You can't. This place doesn't let the rooms. Just what you see here … a bar and a café. Now, do you, or do you not, want anything else?"

"Err, nothing else please," says Peter, intimidated by the tough sounding waitress. "Thanks very much."

"Right, well, drink up kids and be on your way," says the waitress, over her shoulder, as she saunters back to her place behind the counter, adding, "… believe me, you really don't want to be hanging about in this creepy old place."

Sipping their drinks slowly, to make them last longer, the Warriors *do* hang about, for almost an hour. Fed up, and wondering if they might have made a mistake, they

are debating whether to give up and go home, when the
hotel doors swing open, and in walks the vile woman.
Following close behind her, the shell suit man is carrying a
huge holdall, carefully, as if it was really fragile. They are
accompanied by a large, round man dressed in a dark grey,
three-piece suit.

"I know him," says Noah. "That's Councillor Beattie.
What's he doing here? He tried to chop down my tree. He
hates me. Oh no, don't let him see me." Snatching up a
greasy menu, Noah holds it to his face.

"Get this place cleaned, you lazy, good-for-nothing
slob," the vile woman shouts through the café door before
disappearing up the stairs with the two men. The scowling
waitress picks up a dirty tea towel and mutters, pretending to
wipe the counter before slipping her phone out of her pocket
and retreating into the kitchen.

"This old place is fantastic, Pete," says Noah, taking out his
phone and photographing the old fashioned fittings and tiles,
but Peter isn't listening. He is watching Jet.

"Jet … are you okay?" he asks.

"Fine …" says Jet, looking slowly around the group.
"Where's Polly? I think we need to stay together in this
place."

"Loo, I think," says Angela, adding, "… is everything all
right, Jet? You don't look well."

"Right … come on," says Josh, as the kitchen door closes
behind the waitress, "… up the stairs, quick, let's follow
them."

Completely forgetting that Noah is in a wheelchair, the
Warriors run out of the café and follow Josh to the upper
floors. Disgruntled, Noah has no choice but to wait behind
in the dingy hotel lobby, and he busies himself taking
photographs of a multi-coloured bottle window that is set
into the back of a dark little alcove. Moving in for a close up,
Noah is shocked when, through the thick swirled glass, he
spots Polly, pacing up and down in the supermarket car park.

"I never had you down as a coward, Polly," he thinks.

"Fancy running off and leaving the rest of us to do the dirty work … some warrior you are."

When Peter, Angela and Jet catch up with Josh, he is crouching outside the half open door of room 209, at the end of a long draughty corridor on the second floor. From the crack in the doorway, a sliver of dull yellow light casts a long thin shard on the faded threadbare carpet. Putting a finger to his mouth, Josh signals to them to be very quiet and then points to the room.

"They're in here," he mouths, theatrically, not making a sound.

Peter and Jet crouch behind Josh, but Angela creeps around them, positioning herself just out of the light, so that she can see straight into the bedroom. Pointing her phone at the opening in the doorway, she presses the record button and then freezes, terror-stricken, as the shell suit man gets up from his chair and starts towards her.

"Leave that door open, you idiot," says the vile woman. "This place stinks of damp. Do you me want to suffocate?"

"Yes, my love," murmurs the shell suit man, through his teeth, before forcing a smile, turning and then walking back into the room, saying, loudly, "anything you say … my love."

"God, you make me sick," says the vile woman, as she turns back to the councillor and asks, "so … how much do you want for the licence?"

"That depends on how much they are worth," says Councillor Beattie. "Do you have one with you?"

"Show him!" says the vile woman.

Jumping to attention, shell suit man reaches into the holdall and lifts out a tiny body that is completely wrapped up in a fleece blanket. Through the crack in the door, Angela watches him placing the body on the table, and she notices that he takes a great deal of care to make sure that it is safe and well covered.

"There you are my precious girl … you'll soon have a new mummy and daddy," he says, adding, "I've given her a sedative, so she won't wake up for ages."

"This nappy is stinking," says vile woman. "I thought I told you to change that."

Listening from the corridor, the Warriors are shocked.

"It's a baby," mouths Angela, moving her arms to and fro, as if she is rocking an infant to sleep.

"They're selling children?" mouths Peter, looking at Jet and Josh in utter despair.

"Oh, no," mouths Jet, wide eyed, hands flying up to her cheeks. "What are we going to do?"

Lost for words, Josh can only raise his shoulders and shake his head.

Squatting perfectly still, Angela keeps her eyes fixed on the fleece, which moves slightly as the little figure inside it begins to wriggle.

"There's plenty more where that came from," says the vile woman. "We got a delivery last night … plucked from their families less than a week ago. Half of them were dead in the truck, of course. Useless bloody traffickers. I said to them, that's my profit you're messing with, I said, but they don't give a hoot."

The little body in the fleece stretches, his legs pushing against the fabric, which falls open, giving Angela a clear view of the tiny creature that is hidden inside it.

"Monkeys!" she screams, springing up and crashing into the bedroom. "They're selling bloomin' monkeys."

Snatching up the drowsy little animal, Angela turns towards the door, but the shell suit man steps in front of her, blocking her exit. Turning in all directions, Angela frantically scans the room, but there is no escape. She is trapped.

"Give me back my investment," says the vile woman, ripping the monkey from Angela's hands. "I paid good money for these damn things."

Waking up, the frightened squirrel monkey lashes out, her fingernails clawing at the skin on the vile woman's hand.

"Arrgh! The wretched thing attacked me," she screeches, throwing the animal away and grasping the wound to stop the blood.

In a blur, the little monkey runs out of the door, shoots past the bewildered Warriors, and heads down the corridor, making straight for an open window. Then, to their amazement, she suddenly scrambles to a halt, changes direction and runs towards the stairwell. Only Jet can see the shimmering balloon of white pulsing light, filled with tiny silver sparklers, that has positioned itself in front of the window.

"Guardian angel! Is that you? Where have you been?" cries Jet, jumping to her feet and haring towards the stairs in pursuit of the monkey, calling over her shoulder. "Thank you … thank you for helping us."

"Did she say guardian angel?" whispers Peter, but Josh is also on his feet.

"We need to help Angela," he says. "Come on."

The boys crash into the bedroom where they find Angela tied to the radiator. But with no clue as to what they should do next, they hesitate, giving the vile woman time to rummage in her handbag, and then point a small pink pistol directly at Angela's forehead. At the same time, the shell suit man pulls a gun from a holster under his track suit and prepares to fire. Stopping in their tracks, the boys slowly raise their hands.

"I can't be seen here," says Councillor Beattie, grabbing his papers and hurrying out of the door. "Keep my name out of this."

Walking briskly the councillor heads down the stairs, faltering for a moment when he reaches the first floor, where the little monkey has attached herself to a newel post and Jet is balanced on the edge of a step, arms outstretched, trying to catch him.

Deciding to ignore them, the councillor continues down the stairs and into the lobby, where he finds Noah blocking his escape route. Quickly shoving Noah's wheelchair into the alcove, he turns towards the door and spots a policeman standing across the street. Spinning on his heel, the councillor strides into the café, grabs a discarded newspaper and sits at a table, breathing deeply to calm himself down. Flicking the broadsheet paper open, he buries his head in its pages: pretending to be an innocent customer.

At the top of the stairs, Jet makes a grab for the monkey, but she is too slow. Shrieking in terror, the animal loses her grip, slides down the banister and lands on Noah just as he is manoeuvring his wheelchair, backwards, out of the alcove. Feeling a tiny hand grabbing at his clothes, Noah spins his chair in every direction, trying to shake the thing off. When the hand grabs the back of his hair he flies into a blind panic.

"Whoa! It's the demon. GET OFF ME! GET OFF ME!" he yells.

Turning the wheel rims with all of his strength, Noah shoots out of the hotel door, ending up in the middle of the crossroads, spinning his chair and bringing the traffic to a standstill.

Jet's shoulders drop and she stands in the doorway, watching Noah's antics, thinking, "Oh, well, that's just great." Then, gathering her wits about her, she follows him into the street.

"It's a monkey, Noah," she shouts, from the kerb. "She's a little monkey. Catch her … you wuss!"

At the sound of Jet's voice, Noah stops spinning his chair. Losing her grip, the little monkey flies round and lands on his lap. Petrified, the animal clings to him. Suddenly realising his mistake, Noah secures the monkey inside his jacket before making his way off the crossing, leaving behind an uproar of confused policemen, hooting cars, and irate drivers shouting at him to clear off.

A second later, Polly emerges from the supermarket car park with PC Dally at her back. They reach the hotel door just in time to hear a gunshot fired, and the blood curdling scream of a female voice filling the air.

"Angela's still up there!" shouts Jet.

"Wait here," says PC Dally, taking the stairs two at a time. Disobeying his order, Polly follows him, stopping briefly at the café door to see Councillor Beattie speaking with two police officers. Then she sprints up the stairs to room 209 where she finds the vile woman sitting on the floor holding a disposable nappy to a bloody, injured, hand. The pink pistol is lying by the window, out of her reach, and shell suit man is on his knees, untying Angela.

"Who the hell are you?" he is shouting at the Warriors. "Eighteen months of hard work, and you lot have ruined it in five minutes. I almost had them."

"YOU!" says the vile woman. "You pathetic little ..."

"Shut up," says shell suit man, flashing his police badge. "You're under arrest."

PC Dally looks sideways at shell suit man.

"David?" he says, "What are you doing here? What's going on?"

"Eustace?" says shell suit man, "I've been doing undercover work. Wild animal traffickers ... and I almost had them until this flaming lot turned up."

"It's Councillor Beattie," says Peter, rushing towards PC Dally. "He's the Mr Big in all of this. He wanted money to grant a licence to this really vile woman."

"He cleared off when we arrived," says Josh, pushing in front of Peter. "I don't know where he went to, but it was definitely him."

"Yes, Polly told me he was here," says PC Dally, putting a hand up to keep the excited boys at bay. "Don't you worry about him."

"We've got proof," says Angela, proudly. "We recorded everything. We did, didn't we guys?"

"Now, why doesn't that surprise me," says PC Dally, flashing a sideways smile at the shell suit policeman.

"Are we going to get into trouble, Constable Dally?" asks Polly, genuinely worried about what her parents will say. "We were only trying to investigate; we thought they were breeders; we didn't realise how serious it was."

"You shouldn't go getting involved in matters that don't concern you, Polly," says PC Dally. "But, no, leave it with me.

I'll sort it out. Only … don't do it again. Am I making myself clear enough this time?"

"We won't," says Polly, crossing her fingers behind her back and adding, "… will we, guys?"

"Mr Big?" says Josh, looking at Peter and shaking his head. "Where on earth did you get that from?"

"*The Detectives!*" says Peter. "On TV … don't you guys watch anything interesting?"

The two policemen escort the vile woman, now in handcuffs, out of the building. With her face set in a horrible scowl, the woman is pushed past Noah and Jet, who are in the lobby, fussing over the cute little monkey.

"I'll take this little one now," says the shell suit policeman, as Noah reluctantly hands the animal to him. "She and the others will be taken to a squirrel monkey sanctuary in Brazil. They belong in the tropical rain forests."

"Can't you take them back to their families?" asks Polly.

"Sadly, no," says the shell suit policeman. "It's too late for that. But they'll be together at the sanctuary, and it is their natural habitat. That's the best we can do for them after they've been trafficked like this."

"Who would want to keep a squirrel monkey as a pet anyway?" asks Angela. "I mean, it's illegal for a start."

"Actually, it's not," says the shell suit policeman. "Unethical maybe, but not illegal … not yet, anyway. It's something that we're working on."

"We need to influence the law makers," says Josh. "I keep telling them, but they won't listen to me. It's the only way."

The Warriors all roll their eyes.

"Oh, for pete's sake, Josh," says Noah. "Not that again."

But, cuddling the little monkey close to his chest, the shell suit policeman looks at Josh and nods.

"You got that right, son," he says.

Chapter 7

POLITICS

"Do your parents know that you're here?" asks Mr Beadle, as the Warriors file past him and into the dining room, for a debriefing meeting about the squirrel monkeys.

"Yes, Mr Beadle," say the Warriors, in unison, like school assembly.

"Well … I hope you're telling me the truth," says Mr Beadle, dropping some ring-pull tinned vegetables into Peter's shopping trolley, and adding, "Do I need to phone them to check?"

"No, Mr Beadle," say the Warriors, in unison again.

"Right, well, I'm trusting you lot to behave yourselves," says Mr Beadle, who docs not trust them at all, "so let's have no more of your shenanigans, okay!"

"Okay! We get the message, Dad," says Josh, earnestly. "We do … honest!"

Pointing his index finger at nothing and nodding solemnly, Mr Beadle says, "Well … just think on …" before backing out of the room and closing the door.

"What's up with him?" says Noah, bashing his wheelchair against the furniture on the way around the table to his usual place. "We did a good thing and that's all the gratitude we get."

Slumping against the back of his dining chair, Peter sighs and his eyebrows knit together in a frown, as he glances wearily at Noah.

"What?" says Noah, indignantly.

Jet laughs.

"I'm with you, Noah," she says, folding the wheelchair and putting it aside, whilst Noah makes himself comfortable on the dining chair. "I'm quite proud of what we did."

"It was really exciting," says Polly, her face bright and animated. "And I think we should do it again."

"What we need to do," declares Josh, confidently, his hands waving about as if he was addressing a large rally, "is to get our message to the politicians. The Prime Minister! It's the only way. You all heard that policeman in the shell suit ... he agreed with me."

The others stop talking and stare at him.

"Oh, not again, Josh? Are you mad?" says Angela. "You know we can't do that."

"What are you all afraid of?" says Josh. "We go to Westminster and take our manifesto into parliament. Why not?"

"Because it's too big, Josh, that's why not!" says Noah, "We should go and picket a puppy farm or a logging factory or ... something."

"No, Josh is right," says Jet. "Picketing doesn't do any good. We need to go and speak to the law makers in person. Isn't that right, Josh?"

"Well ... if you don't ask ... you don't get! That's my motto," says Josh. "Trust me, it'll be fine. Piece of cake!"

"My mum will go nuts," says Angela, whispering to Polly.

"Mine too," says Polly, then, mimicking Josh, "... 'be fine' ... 'piece of cake'."

The girls burst out laughing.

"We can do it," says Josh, frowning at the childishness of their giggles. "We'll take the train to Westminster and hand our manifesto to the Prime Minister. How can that be so hard?"

"Errm ... what if the police get involved again?" mutters Noah, his bravado deserting him. "We'll definitely go to prison this time. I don't think I'd be able to manage in a prison."

Nobody is listening to Noah because they are poring over Josh's notes and diagrams, totally immersed in the excitement of their new plan. Wondering if they have ramps in prison, Noah gazes, despondently, at the trees in Josh's garden, until Peter asks him a question.

"Hmm, what?" says Noah, blinking: pulling his gaze away from the greenness of the garden, "Do what?"

"Create a diversion at Westminster," says Peter, matter-of-factly.

"Me! Create a diversion? How? Why me?" says Noah, suddenly realising that they are all looking at him: a tingle of panic rising in his stomach.

Peter's body stiffens and he leans on the glass table, his hands pressing with such force that his fingertips are turning white.

"It's not that big a deal, Noah," he says, exasperated. "You only have to fall out of your wheelchair in the entrance hall … and Jet will be with you. I mean, it's the rest of us who'll be taking all the risks."

"WHAT!" exclaims Noah, his head pulling back, like a cobra ready to strike. "Have you all gone mad? Why would I do THAT!"

"You haven't heard a thing we've been saying, have you?" says Peter. "You only have to …"

"Fall out of my wheelchair, yes, I heard you!" says Noah, raising his voice. "Pete, how could you even think I would do that?"

"Oh, for heaven's sake, Noah," snaps Peter. "It's the only way we can distract the guards. No one can resist helping a kid in a wheelchair, you know that! You use that tactic all the time. You know it works."

"He is right about that," says Noah, looking around the table, at the eager faces of the other Warriors. "It does work and, yes, I have found it useful at times. But … in Parliament? I don't know, guys."

Jet starts to snigger.

"You crafty beggar," she says, nudging Noah. "What a hoot."

The others laugh, but Noah does not join in.

"Do it, Noah," says Polly, egging him on. "We really need you."

"It's for the Warrior cause, Noah," says Angela. "You have to do it."

"I'll be right beside you," says Jet, touching his shoulder. "If we go down, we'll go together. Do they have mixed prisons these days?"

"Come on, Noah," says Peter, reassuringly. "You'll have Jet's guardian angel to protect you. Won't he, Jet?"

"What? Oh … err … it doesn't really work like that, Peter," says Jet, remembering her outburst in the hotel corridor and feeling a little foolish.

"But it was there, wasn't it," says Peter, who is genuinely interested. "You spoke to it … I heard you … in that hotel?"

"Well, yes," says Jet, "it was there. But they can't sort everything for us. We're supposed to work things out for ourselves."

"Then, what's the point in having it?" asks Josh, sarcastically, adding, "Surely an angel could bail you out now and again."

"They do," says Jet, "all the time. But if they sort every single mess we make, well, we'd just be like puppets. We have free will."

"I think I might have seen mine," says Peter, relieved to be able to talk about his strange experience. "It helped me when I was hoisting Noah up that tree, and it was blue … definitely blue."

Noah's head snaps around and he stares, disbelieving, at Peter.

"I think mine might be … erm, gold," says Polly, more hesitantly than Peter. "I saw a tower, sort of like golden sunshine, in the school dinner hall, but I didn't know what it was. You saw it too, Angela, didn't you? Is that it, Jet, could that have been my angel?"

Angela says nothing.

"What a load of codswallop!" says Josh, pompously, annoyed that the subject of angels has been brought into his serious discussion about politics. "Can we please leave the mumbo jumbo out of this?"

"It's NOT mumbo jumbo, Josh!" says Jet, frustrated at his closed mindedness. "You might not believe me, but it's true. Every one of us has a guardian ange…"

"No!" says Josh, emphatically, "We don't! Because angels don't exist!"

Polly, Noah, Angela and Peter watch in silence as Jet and Josh lock eye to eye, each challenging the other to back down.

"Okay," says Noah, trying to stop the argument. "Okay, I'll do it. I'll pretend to fall out of my chair, for the Warrior cause."

"Brilliant, Noah," says Peter, glad that the tension has been broken.

"Right then," says Angela, standing up and looking sideways at Polly. "That's settled! I need to get back to the hospital. I have a lot of new animals to see to."

"I'll come with you," says Polly, awkwardly, pushing her chair back and getting to her feet. "if that's all right."

As the others prepare to leave, Jet and Josh remain seated, eyes fixed in an ice-cold, unyielding stare, their reflections frozen in the polished glass table top. Then Josh falters, breaking eye contact, as a ghostly column of the palest green mist, swirling around a deep emerald flame, materialises at his side, slowly rotating like a gentle tornado. The apparition extends fragmented wisps that hang in the air around Josh, like breath on a cold winter's day, though he is completely unaware.

Letting go of her anger, Jet realises that she actually feels sorry for Josh. She wishes that he could believe, at least in his own guardian angel, which is trying so hard to break through.

"*Help him,*" she thinks, urging the angel to nudge Josh, just a little bit harder. "*He is missing so much.*"

"Right then," says Polly, shattering the moment as she slips her arm into her coat sleeve. "Well … we're all going now, Josh."

"Are you coming, Jet?" says Peter. "My mum's doing a curry at her Thai cookery class and she says that you can come for lunch, if you like."

"Hmmm? Oh, yes …" says Jet, breaking her train of thought and turning her attention to Peter, "… yes, thanks Pete. That sounds great."

"So," says Josh defiantly, his eyes scanning the group whilst, unbeknown to him, the angel-mist fades and then dies away, "are we agreed? We take our solid, physical, real-life manifesto to Westminster next week."

"Oooh, yes," says Polly, nudging Angela.

"We can't wait," says Angela.

"And I'll practice the fall from my chair … to sweet perfection," says Noah, making an a-okay sign with his thumb and index finger.

"Great," says Josh, glancing briefly over the table at Jet, who, having calmed down, is getting ready to leave. "I'll check the dates and times, and then text everyone. Is everybody okay with that?"

"Sure," says Jet, slipping her arm into the sleeve of her jacket as, without looking back, she heads out of the door, behind Peter.

✳ ✳ ✳ ✳ ✳

On the morning of the expedition to Westminster, the Warriors meet at the train station for a breakfast of potato crisps and hot chocolate. Having assumed the role of leader, Josh has already bought the tickets, collected a timetable, completed the virtual tour of the Houses of Parliament and made diagrams of the route through the building.

"Did you practice your fall, Noah?" asks Jet, who is still avoiding eye contact with Josh.

"Of course," says Noah. "I spent the whole week falling out of my wheelchair. I'm fairly sure I can make it look like an accident."

"Right, this is what we'll find when we get there," says Josh, handing a diagram to each of them. "Our train comes in at platform six. We'd better look for an assistant for you Noah. Come on."

The train flies through a blur of fields and houses, ripping across the countryside, speeding the anxious Warriors towards London. They hardly say a word because, apart from Polly, who is staring out of the window and wondering what her mum will do when she finds out, each Warrior is trying to memorise their diagram of the corridors through which they will be passing, later in the day.

"We need to get this right first time, guys," says Josh, his words hanging heavy in the air around them, "because there will be no second chance."

The London Underground is a challenge for Noah in his wheelchair. Waiting for guards to help him on and off trains, and looking for the lifts between platforms frustrates him, and it delays the Warriors, who don't have time to waste.

When they finally arrive at the Houses of Parliament, they are surprised to find that it has an airport style body-scanner, and some very serious looking security people, who are checking tickets at the door. The Warriors hadn't expected that. Their invasion is doomed to fail before it even starts. Unsure what to do next they hang about on the pavement watching a line of tourists zig-zagging along the queue barrier like a giant centipede.

"I thought you said this would be easy," says Angela, looking at Josh, "… 'piece of cake' you said."

Josh shrugs, casually.

"We won't get past that lot, Josh." says Peter, "You brought us all the way here, and we can't even get into the building."

"Why would they stop six kids, with one in a wheelchair," says Josh, who is in his element and not the least bit bothered by the security, "It'll be fine. Just stay calm."

"We could just go to the science museum instead," says Polly, hopefully. "Have a day out on London … now that we're here."

"No," says Jet. "We need to get in there somehow; we have a job to do, remember? We're supposed to be the Indigo Warriors."

"Well, at least there aren't any steps," says Noah, fed up with the effort of getting around London, and quite looking forward to manoeuvring his wheelchair around the tight corners of the winding barrier.

They are considering what to do next when Josh spots a large group of chattering, animated school children pouring out of a school bus. They gather on the pavement a little way along the road.

Struggling to control her pupils, the young teacher gives up trying to count heads and simply steers them, haphazardly, towards the entrance ramp.

"Everybody ... stay with me," the teacher is shouting, her voice drowned out by the noise of London traffic. "The workshop starts in forty-five minutes, so you'll have time to look around the main hall."

"Right," says Josh, "it's everyone for himself. We'll tag onto this class, get inside and then meet up again in the hall. Good luck everybody. Let's go."

"Wait a minute, Josh," says Peter, "they'll see us walking over ..."

"NOW!" says Josh getting to his feet and trotting towards the crowd.

Dispersing themselves amongst the school children and keeping their heads down, the Warriors inch their way towards the scanner. Then, out of the blue, a short, stout visitor assistant in a tight uniform that strains at every button hole, takes a long, suspicious look at Polly before putting a hand up, to stop her.

"Excuse me, young lady," says the visitor assistant. "Are you, by any chance, with this group?"

"Erm ... yes, miss," says Polly, who, uncomfortable at telling a bare-faced lie, is sure that her cheeks are turning bright red. She looks around for Angela, who is just going through the scanner and into the building. To her horror, Polly spots all the other Warriors inside. She is that last one. She is on her own.

"Right," says the visitor assistant, "well, see that you keep up with your class today, and for heaven's sake don't get yourself lost, okay. Stragglers will not be tolerated."

"I will, I mean ... I won't ... I mean," says Polly, choking with nerves, "I'd … um … better catch them up … um, thank you."

Keeping her head bowed, and walking as steadily as she can with tense locked knees, Polly allows herself to be guided through the security scanner. A visitor's badge, in a plastic holder, is hung around her neck, and she makes her way through the crowd, towards the rest of the group, who are waiting by the reception desk.

"Oh my lord, that was close," she says, shaking with excitement, as she joins the others. "I can't believe it. We're in!"

"How can you be enjoying this, Polly?" asks Peter. "My nerves are in pieces."

"It's only an adventure, Pete," says Polly, shrugging cheerfully. "I mean … what's the worst that could happen?"

"We could all go to jail, Polly," replies Noah, emphatically. "That's what could happen."

"Look at this place," says Angela, tilting her head to look up at the royal statues, embedded in the walls of Westminster Hall. "Isn't it beautiful."

"It's bloomin' enormous," says Noah, gazing at the high, vaulted ceiling and sighing. "Makes me feel quite small."

"This is the home of democracy," says Josh, overwhelmed by the experience. "It's my … spiritual home."

"*No, it isn't, Josh,*" thinks Jet. "*Your spiritual home is more wonderful than you could ever imagine.*"

When he sees the wide stone steps he will need to negotiate to get up to the central lobby, Noah groans.

"Oh, for heaven's sake, not again," he mutters, preparing to flip himself out of the wheelchair and onto the bottom step. "I'll just …"

"DON'T!" says Peter, putting a hand on Noah's shoulder to keep him in his chair. "What are you doing? You're supposed to be the poor disabled boy, remember? For pete's sake, Noah, keep up, will you!"

"What? Oh yeah," says Noah. "I forgot about that."

Deciding to carry him up the steps by themselves, the

Warriors gather round, and are just taking hold of the wheelchair when, to their horror, they see a tall, burly visitor assistant striding briskly towards them.

"What's going on here?" asks the deep voice of the assistant, who is eyeing Noah's wheelchair suspiciously. "What are you lot up to?"

"We're going to carry our friend up the steps," says Josh, as confidently as he can manage.

"Oh, are you now?" says the visitor assistant, raising one eyebrow, "Well, I'm afraid you will not be doing that today, my boy."

"Won't we?" says Josh, working hard to keep his voice steady.

"No son. You need to use the lift. Here, let me help you along there, sonny," says the man, elbowing Josh out of the way, taking charge of Noah's wheelchair and pushing him towards the lift doors, calling, "Follow me kids."

Choking back the urge to laugh at Noah's predicament, the Warriors fall into line behind the assistant. Noah, who never allows anyone to push him about, and absolutely hates it when people talk down to him just because he is in a wheelchair, grits his teeth. Smiling, he clasps his hands on his lap as the assistant shoves his chair into the lift and pulls on the brakes, leaving Noah facing the mirrored back wall of the carriage.

"Thank you very much for helping me," says Noah, to the assistant's reflection in the mirror.

"You're very welcome, sonny," says the visitor assistant, leaning right across Noah's head and messing up his hair, to push the button for the upper floor.

"Enjoy your visit, kids," continues the assistant, cheerily. "And, mind now, stay out of trouble."

"Thank you, sir, we will," says Josh.

Shuffling about and coughing under their breath, the Warriors wait for the lift doors to close, and then immediately fall about, howling with laughter.

"All right there ... SONNY," says Peter, ruffling Noah's hair even more.

"Shurrup!" says Noah, ducking to avoid Peter's hand, until Josh, wiping laughter tears with his tie, says, "SHUSH everybody! Shhh ... this is our floor."

As the lift approaches the upper floor, the Warriors quickly gather their composure so that, when the doors ping open, they emerge quiet and unnoticed. Then they split up.

Noah and Jet make their way to the far end of the huge hall, and the others hang about the entrance to the south corridor, pretending to look at the statues. Josh checks the information on the video screens.

"They sit at two thirty. That gives us twenty-five minutes," he says. "We need to get in there, right away."

Signalling to Jet, Peter waves across the crowded hall.

Jet nudges Noah, who nods.

"Ready?" asks Jet.

"Here goes nothing," says Noah, flinging himself, noisily, out of his wheelchair and landing on the cold floor tiles.

"Ahhhh," Noah yells, at the top of his voice. "My leg. It's my leg. Ouch ... Ooo." His voice echoing around the big stone walls, he rolls on the floor clutching at his knee, which does, in fact, hurt.

"Oh, no," shouts Jet, "my friend is injured. Somebody help us please."

Just as they had planned it, every head turns until every eye in the place is looking in Noah's direction, as the visitor assistants run over to help him.

"What happened, son?" asks one of the assistants.

"Health and safety," shouts Noah, the actor, who is trying not to laugh. "My wheelchair was tipped over by a loose tile."

"Loose tile? What loose tile?" say the assistants, falling to the floor and running their hands over it, to check for a tile that could have caused the accident.

"Never mind the floor," says Noah, keeping everyone's attention on himself. "Get me up. I'm in pain here, for pete's sake!"

"Oh, sorry son," says one assistant. "Only the first-aider can do that. He'll be here in a minute. You hang in there and be a brave little man, okay?"

Glancing up at Jet, Noah bites his lip and almost laughs out loud.

At the other end of the hall, the rest of the Warriors slip through the heavy swing doors and run down the passageway that leads to the Commons Chamber. The polished tiles in the deserted corridor exaggerate the slightest sound, so that every footstep echoes around them. Feeling confident of their success, the Warriors are almost at the Members' Lobby when they hear voices coming from the other side of some swing doors.

Crashing into one another, they skid to a halt on the polished floor, frantically looking up and down the stark, empty corridor. There is nowhere to hide. Scrambling for the wall beside the doorway, Josh and Polly flatten their bodies against the cold tiles and, assuming that Angela will follow him, Peter dives for the other side.

"I ... I ... ca ... I ... can't ... I ...," Angela freezes in front of the doors: her feet are rooted to the spot.

"Over here," Peter urges her to move. "Quick, Angela, hurry."

Seeing the alarm on Angela's face the others wave hysterically, silently encouraging to her to get beside a door. The female voices are so close that the Warriors can hear them, chatting about a boy who has fallen out of a wheelchair in the hall. Then the hinges squeal. The doors start to open.

The blood drains from Angela's face, and she begins to whimper. All she can do is squeeze her eyes tightly shut and await her fate. In a split second, Peter has grabbed her sweatshirt and pulled her beside him, immediately putting a hand over her mouth, almost suffocating her, so that she can't give them away.

Immediately, two women crash through the polished swing doors, flinging them wide open, concealing the

Warriors behind them. Helpless, they can only wait for the doors to swing straight back and leave them fully exposed. But the hinges seem to stick, jamming both doors open.

Safe in their hiding place, the Warriors wait as the cleaning ladies shuffle along the corridor, complaining about their job and juggling an assortment of buckets and mops, until they crash through the doors to the next corridor, leaving silence in their wake.

Putting both hands flat against the door Polly gives it a hard push, but it is stuck fast and does not move, not even a fraction. Frowning, she turns and looks at Josh, who, open mouthed, simply shrugs.

Behind the other door, Peter releases Angela, who is grateful for a deep breath. Then he puts his head around the door and looks down the corridor to check if the coast is clear. Glancing up he notices that the doors are being held in place by two golf-ball sized spheres of swirling blue light. Nudging Angela, he raises his eyebrows and smiles, as he nods towards the lights.

"Huh? What?" says Angela, looking up but showing no sign of sharing Peter's vision. "What are you looking at?"

Unable to speak, Peter stares at the swirling little balls of energy as they start to fade and then disappear altogether. The moment they have gone, the doors swing back into place and Peter turns to face Angela.

"Oh ... um ... nothing," he says, casually. "It was nothing."

"The doors stuck!" says Josh, "Can you believe that! The bloomin' doors stuck. I mean ... how lucky was THAT!"

"It wasn't luck, Josh," says Peter, remembering the electric blue angel-light that had helped him to hoist Noah up the tree, "I think that might have been a guardia..."

"Come on," says Josh, interrupting Peter's train of thought. "We need to hurry or we'll miss our deadline."

Their self-belief growing by the minute, the Warriors smile at one another before turning to hare down the corridor, towards the House of Commons. On his way through the

Members' Lobby, Josh touches Winston Churchill's lucky statue, and makes a silent wish that the Warriors will get a chance to speak up before they are thrown out, which, he knows, must happen. Finally, they reach the entrance to the Commons Chamber.

Taking quick, shallow, breaths, Peter grasps the door handle and, hesitating for a second, looks, anxiously, at the other Warriors. In her usual defiant way, Angela nods, giving Peter such a boost of confidence that he pulls hard on the heavy door. For a moment all that they can do is to stand there, staring into the magnificent room. Except for Polly, who, fully expecting to be caught the moment they opened the door, has closed her eyes.

"Brilliant! It's empty, come on," says Josh, leading the Warriors into the chamber and up some steps, to a wooden balcony that smells of wood polish and leather. Working quickly, they squeeze themselves between some benches, where they have a clear view of the whole room. His chest swelling with pride, Josh gazes down at the Speaker's chair and the debating table. He sighs.

"I've come home," he says to Polly, who is nearest to him, "I belong here. If we don't go to prison for this, I am going to be a politician when I leave school."

"Really?" says Polly, "You actually want to do this?"

"It's important, Polly!" says Josh, fed up with his friends' lack of enthusiasm for politics.

Crouched in front of a leather bench, the Warriors wait for their moment to pounce. The only sound in the vast, empty, room is the tick … tick … tick of an enormous wooden clock, until a side door opens and a cheerful voice echoes around the chamber.

"'ere, Kev, go up and check the networks, will you, mate?" shouts a workman to his colleague, "They'll be starting soon."

"Right-o, mate," says Kev, lifting a tool bag that rattles as he makes his way towards the stairwell, whilst the other man checks the microphones on the debating table. Paralysed with fear, the Warriors shrink back into the shadow until they are unable to see what is happening on the ground floor. Hardly daring to breathe, they wait until they hear Kev's good-humoured voice announcing, "Job done, mate."

The men gather up a collection of screwdrivers and headphones before leaving by the main doors, which swing back, noisily, behind them. The chamber falls silent … tick … tick … tick, until the clock strikes two thirty. Exactly!

Immediately, the doors fly open and a grey sea of men and women pours into the chamber, a clamour of excited voices filling the room until it feels as if it might explode with sheer energy. MPs take their seats amid the click of high heels, rustling papers, and constant chatter.

Moving out of the shadows, to get a better view, Josh looks down on the MPs from his hiding place in the balcony. He is completely overwhelmed with admiration for them.

"That'll be me one day," he whispers, as much to himself as to anyone else. The other Warriors are less impressed.

"Look at them!" Peter hisses, under his breath, "Fat Cats! They don't care about hungry people. People are sleeping on the streets, for goodness sake."

"Stay calm, Pete," whispers Josh, giving him a thumbs up.

Taking a deep breath, Peter nods and murmurs, "I'm okay."

"Why do we allow these people rule us?" whispers Polly.

"It's called democracy, Polly," whispers Josh, "it's important."

"Well, I can't say I'm impressed," says Angela, a little too loudly, "I mean …"

"Shh," says Josh, "just listen!"

Crouching in the dark, the Warriors hear debate after debate, as they wait for their chance to speak. It seems to go on forever. Angela can feel her muscles starting to stiffen and she fidgets, trying to stretch her legs in the cramped space. Polly feels sick and the dust makes her nose itch so much that she has to stifle a sneeze. Bored with the whole thing, Peter almost nods off. But Josh is enthralled. He would love it, if only he could get the chance to join in the discussions.

Every MP seems to be shouting at the same time. Cries of

"Mr Speaker," "hear, hear" and "order, order," swirl towards the roof, and everything is followed by hoots of sarcastic laughter.

Angela frowns at Polly.

"Bunch of school kids," she says, clearly unimpressed.

"Angela, we need to argue and debate. It's really important," says Josh, his eyes glazing over as he drifts into his usual daydream. In his mind's eye, he is the leader of the opposition with the freedom to question the Prime Minister as much as he likes. By the time Peter notices the blank look that is sweeping over Josh's face, it is far too late to rouse him from his dream.

"Josh, no," he whispers, frantically shaking his head, "... what are you doing! Josh!"

Totally immersed now, Josh really has become the proud Member of Parliament for his home town, and he is in the House of Commons to raise the concerns of his adoring constituents. Before he knows it, he is on his feet, gesturing wildly and leaning over the balcony, waving his glasses in one hand and his manifesto in the other.

"Mr Speaker," he can hear his own voice, shouting somewhere in the distance. "Honourable Gentlemen, and Ladies of course, ha, ha. I have something rather important that I would like to say."

Instantly, the crowded chamber falls silent and every single person in the room is looking up at Josh, who is jerked straight back to reality.

"Oh ... erm ... I ..." he sputters, putting his glasses back onto his nose and stepping away from the rail. "Oh, help."

Taking the lead, Polly stands up beside Josh and curtsies. Angela stands up next, followed by Peter, who says, "Hi," and raises his hand in a casual wave.

"Are there any more of you up there?" asks the Prime Minister, raising her eyebrows, as the chamber erupts and the politicians burst into a roar of raucous laughter.

"No," says Peter, shouting to be heard above the noise, "just the four of us."

The MPs roar even louder, the Prime Minister is asking questions, and dozens of security people, who seem to appear out of thin air, run about all over the place. Before the Warriors can say another word, they are surrounded by six huge men, who are intent on evicting them, as swiftly as possible.

"Where the hell did they come from? How did they get in here? Grab them!" shouts a security man. "Get them out of here. NOW!"

Polly is overcome with the excitement and, unable to breathe, almost faints. Terrified, Josh is rooted to the spot and, for once, his prowess for elegant speech abandons him.

"Oh, man up, Josh, for heaven's sake," Angela shouts at him. "This was your idea. Say something … for pete's sake … say anything!"

"I … I … I …" is all that Josh can say.

Grabbing the frightened Warriors by their clothing, the security guards manhandle them, extremely roughly, into the aisle, forcing them into the open. "Come here you!" "Get over there, you!" "And you, stand here." The conflicting commands confuse the traumatised children so much that they stumble and trip over one another in their efforts to do as they are being told, until Angela has had enough.

"Oh, for heaven's sake, keep your hair on, you morons!" she shouts at the top of her voice, her words echoing all around the chamber. "We only came to speak to the Prime Minister."

By now the MPs are convulsed with laughter, thoroughly enjoying the entertainment. Mortified and furious that some children have managed to get past their security measures, the red faced guards are dragging the Warriors along the aisle when the Prime Minister puts up a hand to stop them.

"Wait! Let these young people speak," she says, waving up to the balcony and adding, "come down here, children, where we can all see you."

This is the chance they have waited for.

The chance of a lifetime.

With an abruptness that shocks the Warriors, the MPs stop laughing, and the chamber falls completely silent. Unsure of themselves, the guards glance at one another before releasing the Warriors and standing aside, waiting for the Prime Minister to give them further instructions.

Angela moves first.

The others follow her lead, and they make their way, single file, along the aisle, down the steps and into the House of Commons Chamber. At last the Indigo Warriors find themselves standing in front of the Government. It is precisely as Josh had imagined it.

Bending her knees in another low curtsy, Polly holds the Warriors' manifesto in her outstretched hand. Towering over her, the Prime Minister takes the sheet of paper and her eyes move quickly from side to side, scanning the page, giving the impression that she is reading it.

Angela gives her copy to the leader of the opposition who puts on his glasses and, knitting his eyebrows together, carefully inspects every single word that Josh has written. Josh and Peter pass copies of the manifesto around the other MPs, who are just reading them when the door opens and a security guard escorts Jet and Noah into the chamber.

"I found another two in the Lobby," says the guard. "I thought I'd better bring them in, where we can keep an eye on them."

Looking up, the Prime Minister flicks her hand, calling the children forward before dropping the manifesto, dismissively, onto the debating table. Glancing sideways at Noah, who is grinning and giving a thumbs-up, Josh takes a deep breath and begins to explain the Indigo Warriors' plan for a better life.

"Well, you see," he says, his confidence returning, "we believe that, to live a happier life, people really need to ..."

Josh's voice fills the whole chamber and by the time he is finished the MPs are on their feet, cheering and applauding. The stony faced Prime Minister raises an eyebrow and her eyes almost cross themselves when she looks down her nose at the Warriors.

"I will think about your concerns, children," she says, "but I can make no promises. You do understand, don't you? Perhaps when you are a little older …"

The end of the Prime Minister's sentence is drowned out by the roar of applause from a commons chamber full of local MPs. Cries of "Well done, children," "hear, hear," and "what d'you mean 'can't make any promises'?" erupt from the MPs, as the Warriors are led out of the chamber, surrounded by security guards. The exhausted children are thankful when the doors close behind them, muffling the voices and leaving the MPs to debate the Warriors' ideas.

"I'm starving," says Noah, brushing his wheelchair past one of the guards and narrowly missing his toes, "oh, sorry, mister."

"What was all that bowing about?" asks Angela, turning to Polly, "she's not the bloomin' queen, you know."

"Do you think she'll do anything?" asks Jet, throwing the question out to anyone.

"Nope," says Peter, "I think they'll have a good laugh at our expense and then forget all about us."

"That's unfair," says Josh, "you can't know that. Someone might take it seriously. You never know."

Waving goodbye to the security men, the Warriors leave the Houses of Parliament by the main entrance. But, as soon as they open the doors, camera flashes blind them, and a cheer goes up from a huge crowd. Someone shouts, "There they are!" and the roar becomes deafening. Confused, the Warriors hesitate in the doorway. Overwhelmed and frightened, Polly squeezes her eyes shut, her hands immediately covering her ears to block the noise.

Josh lets out a sigh.

"Cameras!" he says, shouting above the noise. "There are cameras in parliament. That's what those workmen were doing. We've been on the television the whole time."

"We did it!" says Angela, pulling Polly's hands away from

her ears. "We got our message out. I said we would! I did, didn't I, Pol?"

"We did? Woohoo, we did it!" says Polly. "We only bloomin' well did it."

Flinging his arms open, Peter wraps them around Jet and lifts her off the ground, swinging her around, in a bear hug. Josh and Noah look at each other. Noah opens his arms for a hug just as Josh offers his hand and they share an embarrassingly public, awkward handshake. A scrum of reporters runs forward, crowding around the children, pushing and jostling to get the exclusive first interview with the famous Indigo Warriors.

"This way, miss," says a man, waving a camera high above his head and snapping non-stop.

"No, this way …," shouts a woman with a microphone, stepping in front and elbowing the man out of the way. "Tell us … just who are these Indigo Warriors?"

"You then, son," says the man, stepping in front of the woman again, and shoving his camera in Noah's face.

"Would you like to comment, love … anything to say … anything at all?" another reporter pushes a microphone at Jet's mouth, pestering her to say something, but she is looking at Peter, too shocked by his hug, to even notice.

In the jam-packed street, behind the media free-for-all, the Indigo Warriors' supporters surge across the road and the besieged children retreat back into the safety of the building.

"How are we going to get home?" says Polly. "We'll never get through this crowd."

"Wait here," says Josh, looking around for a quiet corner. "I'll phone my dad. He'll know what to do."

When he answers the phone, Josh's dad sounds very, very unhappy.

"Dad, it's me," says Josh, "I'm …"

"I already know where you are," his dad interrupts him.

"You do?"

"I do, and so does your mum, and the street, and the rest of the flaming country by the look of it," says Mr Beadle. "You've been all over the news, Josh."

"Oh, of course," says Josh. "Err … dad … I …"

"I'm not angry with you, Josh," says Mr Beadle, sounding very angry indeed. "I'm just glad that you are all safe. I've spoken to the police AGAIN and PC Dally has arranged for a car to bring you all home."

"Thanks, Dad. Sorry, Dad," says Josh, sheepishly.

"Well, we can talk about it when you get home," says Mr Beadle. "This is what I need you to do, right now! Tell the others to call their parents, and ask them to come to our house to pick up their children. Can I trust you to do that much, Josh?"

"Yes, Dad," says Josh, flatly. "Sorry, Dad."

Trotting behind the security guards, the children make their way along corridor after corridor, finally emerging in a cobbled back street, where they are bundled into an enormous car with a little Union Jack flag on the front, and blacked out, bullet proof, windows. No one notices the Warriors escape, as the smiling guards wave them off, and the chauffeur speeds them away, towards home and their families.

When the car finally turns into Josh's quiet little street, his shoulders droop, and he lets out a heartfelt sigh. Scanning the faces of his fellow Warriors, he can see his own uneasiness being reflected back at him. Not a single word passes between the children as they pile out of the car and gather on the pavement. Josh's neighbours peek around twitching net curtains, trying to catch a glimpse of the Indigo Warriors, as the car roars away.

"I wonder how much trouble we are in," says Angela, chewing her bottom lip.

"My dad is going to go ape," says Polly, heavily.

"My dad's usually okay," says Noah, "but my mum … Hell's bells …"

Peter and Jet exchange a secret smile because they know that neither of their parents will be the least bit bothered by their actions.

There are no angel-lights around the children, who do not

feel remotely like warriors when they make their way through the front door and along the narrow hall, with their heads down, fully expecting a stern telling off.

But it doesn't happen.

Huddled in the doorway, the Warriors look blinkingly around the living room, hardly able to believe their eyes. Everyone has come to welcome the heroes, and they all start talking at once.

Polly's parents have brought Mrs Jones and Benjamin, Peter's mum has brought PC and Mrs Dally, Angela's parents have brought Cheryl, the volunteer wildlife nurse and, to Noah's dismay, his parents have brought Esther, who is already on the floor, in a tantrum. Noticing that her mum is not in the room, Jet is disappointed but not surprised, though she had hoped that, perhaps, just this once …

"I'm really sorry, Jet," says Josh's dad, taking her aside and speaking quietly. "Mrs Fairchild did call them, but …"

"Yeah, no worries," says Jet, who really doesn't mind because she has her Warrior friends now, and she is glad about that.

Questions are asked, Mrs Beadle's food is eaten and champagne toasts are drunk until, too tired to think any more, the Warriors slump, pale and subdued, onto the sofa, rubbing their drooping eyelids. Busy enjoying each other's company, the adults hardly notice their exhausted children, until Mrs Dally nudges her husband.

"Time to go home, I think," says the policeman, prompting the families to collect coats and jackets. "It's been a long and eventful day for these exceptional young people."

With everyone talking over one another, and the adults promising to keep in touch, the friends say goodbye and prepare to make their way to their respective homes. Except for Jet, who is invited to Peter's mum's house for a dinner of chilli-non-carne that she made in her vegetarian cookery class.

Then it is all over. The Warriors have completed their mission. The world has heard what they had to say.

"I feel a bit weird," says Noah, sliding his hands into his gloves and taking hold of the wheel rims. "I mean … is that it … is that all we had to do?"

"There's a lot more to be done," says Polly, pulling on her coat.

"I want to carry on," says Angela, helping her with the sleeve.

"But what else could we do?" asks Peter, glancing at Jet.

"Another campaign?" says Jet, hopefully.

"I'm too tired to even think about that," says Noah, "what do you think, Josh?"

Josh isn't tired at all. He is so fired up that he can hardly sit still because, for the first time in his life, he knows that children really do have the power to change things. To make the world a better place, for everyone.

As the famous Indigo Warriors trudge wearily down the gravel drive, Josh crosses his fingers and calls after them:

"Same time next week?"